SHADOWS OF REALITY SHARON PAZ

Content

Angelika Richter

Imagination and Remembrance
The Silhouettes of Sharon Paz

A female figure at a table slowly inserts a long object into her mouth and begins to eat it. Her mirror image opposite does the very same thing, but in the reverse order and removes the swallowed object whole from her mouth. The looped scene is represented in negative film images. The two figures, the chairs, and the table are bright, while the background remains dark. Sharon Paz's early work entitled *Eating and Re-Eating* (1998), which she created while a student at New York's Hunter College, is one of many from this period where the artist deals with existential and sensual aspects. Mostly using her own body as a medium and a material, she engages in these works in simple everyday acts like eating, *Kissing* (1999) and *Peeing* (1999)— two more of her early videos. The minimalist interventions and their presentation in a simple, stark black-and-white aesthetic that recalls the appearance of photograms are an expression of the expansion of the self-portrait using film. But they point beyond purely artistic self-reflection by including the research of the body viscerally and anticipating all the qualities revealed in Paz's complex performances and video installations today.

The title of her 1998 video work reflects and underscores the moment of the repeating act on a linguistic level, an act that by way of its multiplication and its recurrence in the cycle of images can reveal a quite absurd dimension. The two veterans in wheelchairs sitting opposite each other in *Paralyzed Movement* (2014) are caught in time, in their paralyzed bodies and always repeating the same gestures of rising up. The same is true of the actors in *Restraining Motion*, created that same year, in which as part of the formation of a human chain, not following any recognizable constraints, objects are continuously handed on from person to person and given back. The media-reflexive mirroring of ingesting food in Paz's early video also includes the synchronization of events, spaces, and images that would follow in her later works after completing her studies.

Born and raised in Israel, Sharon Paz comes from a country that is not just shaped by a complex mix of various ethnic backgrounds and religions, but also by numerous armed conflicts that can be traced back to the history of the Holocaust in Germany, the country where the artist lives today. In *The Right to Leave* (2013), Paz links Israeli and German landscapes; in *Open | Close* (2014), Jerusalem's Lions' Gate is associated with depictions of fences that are reminiscent both of various state borders and the entrances to Auschwitz and Buchenwald. The violent occupation and destruction of homes in *Shaded Windows* (2012) and *Sinking Land* (2015) conjure up images of Israel's territorial policy of expansion on the West Bank. At the same time, these are locations, specified in no further detail, that are evoked as metaphors for nation-building, for displacement, and for historic and current wars.

The site-specific performance of *Shaded Windows* doubles the experience of violent conflicts, making them palpable for the audience and moving them directly to the present. In her works, Paz makes the use of different times and local events visible as an artistic intervention and process, while at the same time obfuscating this use. By short-circuiting the various artistic media of video and performance or projecting visual material of a former Jerusalem hospital for leprosy patients onto historical furniture and interiors in *Marks of Existence* (2015), she signals temporal and local fissures.

Paz's early video works depict interior views transported via the body, while her current productions deal with her situation as a migrant and the historical situation of her country of origin and her chosen home; what all her works have in common, however, is their performance character. Actions from her early work, following the tradition of body art, are carried out in the private sphere of the studio. The audience only obtains access to the filmed document. Paz's performances today, always in combination with video projections, sometimes large in format, take place in public as a theatrical event. The actions now are no longer embodied by the artist herself, but by several performers acting at the same time in front of and behind the screen. Bringing together and simultaneously separating filmic image and performance and the layering of several levels of action in the video itself can also be found in the early work discussed at the opening of this essay. Paz moves the artistic action of eating behind a fabric that covers the entire image, transparent enough to make the events visible, but nonetheless covering and veiling them.

The moment of abstraction that leads away from concrete individuals, contexts, and sites of action crystallizes within Paz's early works as negative images, outlines, and cutouts. Since 2009, this has taken place through the appearance of her film figures and that of her performers as black silhouettes. The play of shadows and their visual seductive power reveals only on second glance the artist's critical and political interests. In the first works, which include *The King is Blind* (2011), the filmed and the shadow figures acting in real time both perform before two-dimensional images that in their stark appearance recall the genre of documentary animation. Her later videos are multilayered collages of film whose indexical constitution shows real locations and events. In several of her works, like *We Forgot* (2015), the artist involves viewers in the artistic narrative by allocating them to an active position: either they can interact freely with the figures of the video images or they can follow precise instructions for their actions. In joint shadow play with the filmic schemes, they generate new complexes within processes of negotiating memory culture as the attempt to capture the blind spots of memory.

By using shadows as a visual strategy, Sharon Paz opens a "negative" space of reflection that enables beholders to recognize all sorts of individuals as well as themselves in the undescribed surface of the bodiless shadow, and to project their own visions. Furthermore, the "shadows of reality" in the video and the performance are assigned the function of activating historic and contemporary events and images from the oblivion of forgetting.

Angelika Richter

Imagination und Erinnerung
Die Schattenbilder von Sharon Paz

Eine weibliche Figur an einem Tisch führt langsam einen länglichen Gegenstand in ihren Mund, den sie beginnt zu essen. Ihr spiegelbildliches Gegenüber vollzieht die gleiche Handlung, nur in umgekehrter Abfolge und bringt das geschluckte Objekt in Vollständigkeit aus dem Mund wieder hervor. Die geloopte Szene ist in filmischen

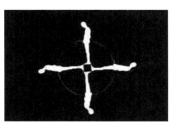

Umkehrbildern dargestellt. Beide Figuren, die Stühle und der Tisch erscheinen hell, der Hintergrund dagegen dunkel. Sharon Paz' frühe, während ihres Studiums am Hunter College in New York entstandene Arbeit mit dem Titel *Eating and Re-Eating* (1998) ist eine von vielen aus dieser Zeit, in denen sich die Künstlerin mit existenziellen und sinnlichen Aspekten befasst. Unter Einsatz zumeist ihres eigenen Körpers als Medium und Material geht sie einfachen Alltagshandlungen wie Essen, Küssen (*Kissing*, 1999) und Urinieren (*Peeing*, 1999) nach. Die minimalistischen Interventionen und ihre Präsentation in einer schlichten, grafischen Schwarzweiß-Ästhetik, die an das Erscheinungsbild von Fotogrammen erinnert, sind Ausdruck für die Erweiterung des Selbstporträts mit filmischen Mitteln. Sie weisen jedoch zugleich über die reine bildkünstlerische Selbstreflexion hinaus, indem sie die Erforschung des Körpers viszeral miteinschließen und indizieren alle Qualitäten, die Paz' heutige komplexe Performances und Videoinstallationen aufzeigen.

Der Titel ihrer Videoarbeit von 1998 reflektiert und unterstreicht auf sprachlicher Ebene bereits das Moment sich wiederholender Akte, die bedingt durch Vervielfältigung und ihre Wiederkehr im Bilderkreislauf eine durchaus absurde Dimension aufweisen können. Gefangen in der Zeit, in ihrem gelähmten Körper und in den immer gleichen, aufbegehrenden Gesten sind die zwei, sich in Rollstühlen gegenübersitzenden Veteranen von *Paralyzed Movement* (2014). Ähnlich ergeht es den Akteur*innen in *Restraining Motion*, entstanden im gleichen Jahr, die sich in der Formation einer Menschenkette – dabei einem nicht erkennbaren Zwang folgend – unablässig Gegenstände von Hand zu Hand weiterreichen und wieder zurückgeben. In der medienreflexiven Spiegelung der Nahrungsaufnahme von Paz' frühem Video ist darüber hinaus die Synchronisierung von Ereignissen, Räumen und Bildern angelegt, die für ihre dem Studium folgenden Arbeiten maßgeblich werden sollte.

In Israel geboren und aufgewachsen, kommt Sharon Paz aus einem Staat, der nicht nur durch eine komplizierte Mischung verschiedener ethnischer Herkunft und Religionen seiner Bürger*innen geprägt ist, sondern vor allem durch zahlreiche kriegerische Konflikte, die im historischen Zusammenhang auf die Geschichte des Holocaust in Deutschland zurückzuführen sind, dem Land, in dem die Künstlerin heute lebt. So verknüpft Paz in *The Right to Leave* (2013) israelische mit deutschen Landschaften, in *Open | Close* (2014) das Jerusalemer Löwentor mit der Darstellung von Zäunen, die sowohl an diverse Staatsgrenzen als auch an die Eingangstore der Konzentrationslager in Auschwitz und Buchenwald denken lassen. Die gewaltsame Besetzung und Zerstörung von Wohnhäusern in *Shaded Windows* (2012) und *Sinking Land* (2015) rufen Bilder der territorialen Expansionspolitik Israels im Westjordanland auf. Zugleich handelt es sich um Schauplätze, die nicht weiter spezifiziert als Metaphern für nationalistische Bestrebungen, Vertreibung, für historische und aktuelle Kriege aufgerufen werden.

Die ortsspezifische Performance von *Shaded Windows* verdoppelt die Erfahrung gewaltsamer Konflikte, lässt sie für das Publikum greifbarer erscheinen und verlagert sie unmittelbar in die Gegenwart. Paz macht den Einsatz verschiedener Zeiten und lokaler Ereignisse in ihren Arbeiten als künstlerischen Eingriff und Prozess sichtbar und verunklärt ihn zugleich. Indem sie die verschiedenen künstlerischen Medien Video und Performance kurzschließt oder Bildmaterial auf historische Einrichtungsgegenstände eines ehemaligen Jerusalemer Hospitals für Lepra-Kranke in *Marks of Existence* (2015) projiziert, zeigt sie zeitliche und lokale Brüche an.

Ungeachtet dessen, dass Paz' Videoarbeiten aus ihrer Anfangszeit als Künstlerin über den Körper transportierte Innensichten wiedergeben, ihre aktuellen Produktionen über ihre Situation als Migrantin und die historische Situation ihres Herkunftslandes und ihrer Wahlheimat erzählen, ist allen Arbeiten ihr Aufführungscharakter gemein. Aktionen aus ihrem frühen Schaffen ereignen sich, der Tradition der Body Art folgend, in der privaten Sphäre des Ateliers. Das Publikum erhält Zugang allein zum filmischen Dokument. Paz' heutige Performances – immer in Verbindung mit ihren mitunter großformatigen Videoprojektionen – finden als theatrales Geschehen in der Öffentlichkeit statt. Die Handlungen werden inzwischen nicht mehr von ihr, sondern von mehreren Darsteller*innen gleichzeitig verkörpert, die vor und hinter der Leinwand agieren. Das Zusammenführen und die gleichzeitige Trennung von filmischem Bild und Performance wie auch die Schichtung von mehreren Handlungsebenen im Video selbst finden sich genauso in der eingangs besprochenen Arbeit angelegt. Die künstlerische Aktion des Essens nämlich verlagert Paz hinter einen aufgespannten, das gesamte Bild ausfüllenden Stoff, der transparent genug ist, das Geschehen sichtbar zu halten, es aber in gleicher Weise verhüllt und verschleiert.

Das Moment der Abstraktion, das von konkreten Personen, Kontexten und Schauplätzen weg führt, kristallisiert sich innerhalb Paz' frühen Arbeiten zu Negativbildern, Umrissen und Cutouts. Seit 2009 geschieht dies durch das Erscheinen ihrer filmischen Figuren und das ihrer Performer*innen als schwarze Silhouetten. Das Spiel der Schatten und ihre visuelle Verführungskraft legen erst auf den zweiten Blick das kritische und politische Anliegen der Künstlerin offen. In den ersten Arbeiten, zu denen *The King is Blind* (2011) gehört, agieren sowohl die gefilmten als

auch die in Realzeit handelnden Schattenfiguren ihrer Performer*innen vor zweidimensionalen Bildern, die von ihrer grafischen Anmutung her an das Genre des dokumentarischen Trickfilms erinnern. Ihre später folgenden Videos sind vielschichtige Collagen filmischer Aufnahmen, die in ihrer indexikalischen Verfasstheit reale Orte und Geschehen anzeigen. Indem die Künstlerin in einigen ihrer Arbeiten wie in *We Forgot* (2015) den Betrachter*innen selbst eine handelnde Position überträgt – entweder können sie frei mit den Figuren der Videobilder interagieren oder folgen genauen Regieanweisungen für ihre Aktionen – sind diese an der künstlerischen Erzählung beteiligt. Im gemeinsamen Schattenspiel mit den filmischen Schemen erzeugen sie neue Zusammenhänge innerhalb erinnerungskultureller Aushandlungsprozesse als Versuch, den blinden Flecken des Gedächtnisses auf die Spur zu kommen.

Durch den Einsatz von Schatten als bildkünstlerische Strategie eröffnet Sharon Paz einen gleichermaßen „negativen" Reflexionsraum, der es den Betrachter*innen ermöglicht, jede denkbare Person darin wiederzuerkennen wie auch sich selbst in der unbeschriebenen Oberfläche des körperlosen Schattens zu imaginieren und eigene Vorstellungen hineinzuprojizieren. Darüber hinaus kommt den „Schatten der Realität" im Video und der Performance die Funktion zu, historische und gegenwärtige Ereignisse sowie ihre Bilder aus dem Dunkel des Vergessens heraus zu aktivieren.

BLIND SPOTS

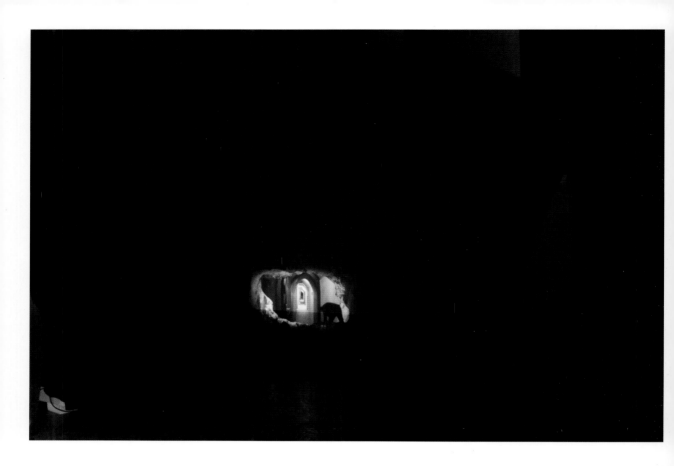

Installation view, KulturRaum Zwingli-Kirche, Berlin, 2016

Installation view, KulturRaum Zwingli-Kirche, Berlin, 2016

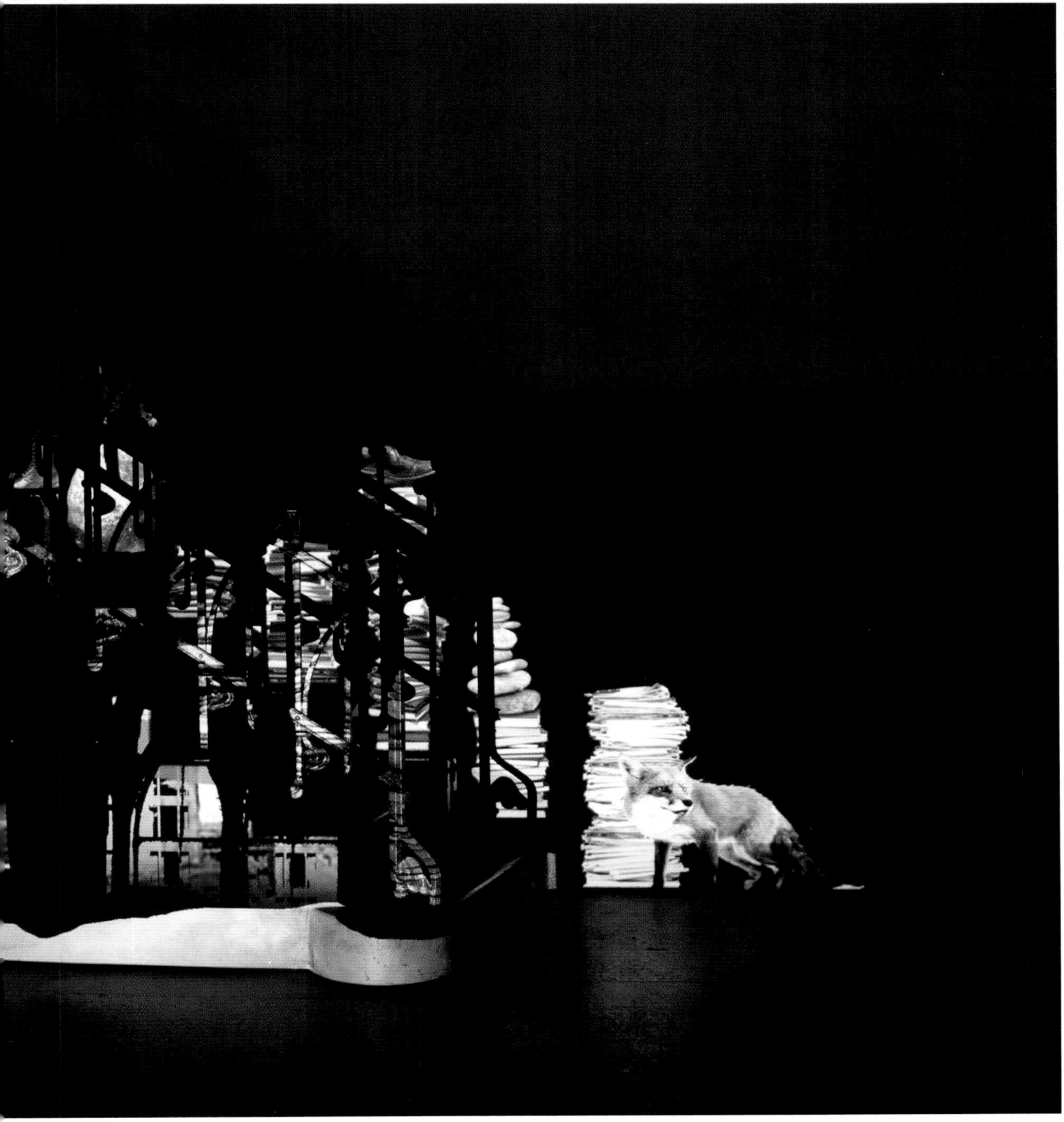

KulturRaum
Zwinstkirdre Berlin

"We kept digging more and more, with bare hands, with cracked fingernails. We dug so deep, so far, that we canceled out the blockade and the borders and the definitions of the upper world. We dug underneath all of that rubbish, and then we kept digging along the length and breadth of the land whose refugees we are. We returned to it, deep down in the earth. We realized a subterranean right of return." Amir Nizar Zuabi

"The Underground Ghetto City of Gaza," in: *Haaretz*, August 4, 2014.
http://www.haaretz.com/opinion/.premium-1.608653

"We kept digging more and more, with bare hands, with cracked fingernails. We dug so deep, so far, that we canceled out the blockade and the borders and the definitions of the upper world. We dug underneath all of that rubbish, and then we kept digging along the length and breadth of the land whose refugees we are. We returned to it, deep down in the earth. We realized a subterranean right of return." *Amir Nizar Zuabi*

"The Underground Ghetto City of Gaza," in: Haaretz, August 4, 2014.
http://www.haaretz.com/opinion/.premium-1.608653

BLIND SPOTS, 2016
Two channel HD video
03:35 min loop

The term "blind spots" is used in psychology to refer to the aspects of a personality that are not recognized by the person in question. The individual's blindness to certain parts of themselves results in a difference between the self and the image others have of us. The site-specific projection on the bottom steps of stairs in front of a church provides insights into imaginary spaces that reveal the hidden and concealed. In the style of Expressionist silent film, fragments of dark and forbidden worlds are illuminated, whereby the lines separating madness and normality are fluid. In certain situations, blind spots can take on an essential protective function as defense and repression.

Als „blinde Flecken" werden in der Psychologie die Seiten einer Persönlichkeit bezeichnet, die von ihr nicht wahrgenommen werden. Durch die eigene Blindheit für gewisse Teile des Ich entsteht eine Differenz zwischen Selbst- und Fremdbild. Die ortsspezifische Projektion auf den unteren Absatz einer Kirchentreppe legt Einblicke in imaginäre Räume frei, die Verborgenes und Untergründiges zu Tage befördern. Im Stil des expressionistischen Stummfilms werden Fragmente düsterer und verbotener Welten beleuchtet, wobei die Grenzen zwischen Wahnsinn und Normalität fließend sind. Situationsbedingt können blinde Flecken als Abwehr und Verdrängung durchaus eine unersetzliche Schutzfunktion übernehmen.

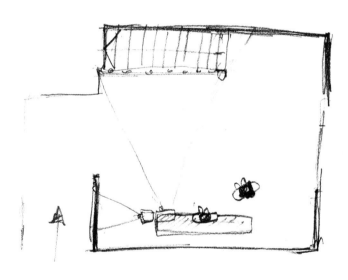

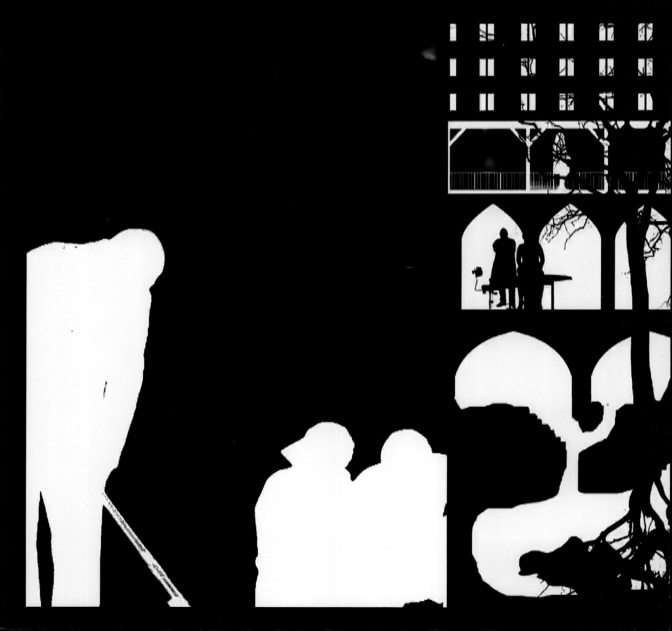

MARKS OF EXISTENCE

Installation view, Hansen House, Jerusalem, 2015

Warehouse

Former Hospital for Leprosy
Hansen House, Jerusalem

"Of all classes, the sick are the most dependent, not just because their bodies are in pain, but because they most acutely depend on the knowledge and good will of another class to relieve their pain: the doctors and their aides. A sick person depends directly, immediately, and totally on the very person who now has quasi-absolute power over his body. A sick person is thus not only weak but also in an acute state of dependency." Eva Illouz

"What the Death of My Father Taught Me About the Demise of Israeli Compassion,"
in: Haaretz, March 14, 2015.
http://www.haaretz.com/israel-news/.premium-1.646583

"Of all classes, the sick are the most dependent, not just because their bodies are in pain, but because they most acutely depend on the knowledge and good will of another class to relieve their pain: the doctors and their aides. A sick person depends directly, immediately, and totally on the very person who now has quasi-absolute power over his body. A sick person is thus not only weak but also in an acute state of dependency." Eva Illouz

"What the Death of My Father Taught Me About the Demise of Israeli Compassion," in: *Haaretz*, March 14, 2015. http://www.haaretz.com/israel-news/.premium-1.646583

MARKS OF EXISTENCE, 2015
Two channel HD video
05:00 min loop

With simple images and minimalist plot, this video installation, consisting of three projections, refers to complex territorial power struggles. Architecture is presented here as a strategy of political intervention and urban warfare. Against a backdrop of buildings of diverse origins and architectural styles, peaceful and violent scenes take place, including a demonstration and patrols that ultimately culminate in the downfall of the hybrid city-state and the violent clearing of the tent city in the foreground. The second large-format projection shows an expanse of water that can be associated with the final collapse of the state, with reference to the myth of the flooding of the belligerent island of Atlantis. In the unequal fight between two individuals, efforts at colonization continue in the foreground of the video. The third part of the work projected onto moving boxes concretizes territorial occupation as invisible strategy: pictures of luxurious villas of a formerly Palestinian part of Jerusalem are shown by Google Street View.

Mit einfachen Bildern und minimalistischen Handlungsabläufen verweist die aus drei Projektionen bestehende Videoinstallation auf komplexe territoriale Machtkämpfe. Architektur wird hier als Strategie politischer Intervention und urbaner Kriegsführung thematisiert. Vor dem Hintergrund einer Häuserkulisse mit Gebäuden unterschiedlicher Herkunft und Bauart finden friedliche und gewalttätige Szenen statt, darunter eine Demonstration und Patrouillen, die letztlich in den Untergang des hybriden Stadtstaates wie auch die gewaltsame Räumung der Zeltstadt im Vordergrund münden. Die zweite großformatige Projektion zeigt einen See, mit dem der endgültige Niedergang des Staates – mit Bezug auf den Mythos von der Überschwemmung der kriegerischen Insel Atlantis – assoziiert werden kann. Im ungleichen Kampf zweier Personen setzen sich im Vordergrund des Videos Kolonialisierungsbestrebungen fort. Der dritte, auf Umzugskisten projizierte Teil der Arbeit konkretisiert territoriale Besetzung als unsichtbare Strategie: Bilder prachtvoller Villen eines ehemaligen palästinensischen Stadtteils von Jerusalem werden darin per Google View aufgerufen.

SINKING LAND

Installation view, Hansen House, Jerusalem, 2015

SINKING LAND, 2015
Three channel HD video
05:00 min loop

This work in several parts refers directly to the history of the exhibition site. Jerusalem's Hansen House was used from the late nineteenth century to the year 2000 as a hospital for leprosy patients and was then transformed into a public cultural center. Outcasts found asylum in this building, received protection and care. As bearers of an illness that was long considered incurable, they were also excluded from society, hidden behind walls and isolated, reduced to their bodies and their frailties by the power of the "clinical gaze" (Michel Foucault). References rich in association in the film and in projections on to the hospital interior evoke the site's past and its patients. At the same time, the visitors to the exhibition are invited to cross the bridge between the past and the present and to become the object under examination.

Die mehrteilige Arbeit bezieht sich unmittelbar auf die Geschichte des Ausstellungsortes. Das Jerusalemer Hansen House diente seit dem Ende des 19. Jahrhunderts bis ins Jahr 2000 als Hospital für Lepra-Kranke und wurde danach in ein öffentliches Kulturzentrum umgewandelt. Aussätzige fanden in diesem Gebäude Asyl, erhielten Schutz und Pflege. Als Träger der lange Zeit nicht heilbaren Krankheit wurden sie zugleich von der Gesellschaft ausgegrenzt, hinter Mauern verborgen und isoliert sowie durch die Macht des „klinischen Blicks" (Michel Foucault) auf ihren Körper und seine Gebrechen reduziert. Assoziationsreiche Bezüge im Film und in Projektionen auf das Krankenhausinterieur rufen die Vergangenheit des Ortes und seiner Patienten auf. Zugleich werden die Ausstellungsbesucher eingeladen, mit ihren Schatten die Brücke zwischen Gegenwart und Vergangenheit zu schlagen und selbst zum Objekt der Betrachtung zu werden.

"I am very concerned about positions that conceive of architecture as an instrument of freedom or repression. In fact, I think that the more you want to get into the act of freeing something, the more you need to look into the abyss of the worst architectural possibilities and into the most intense situations of injustice or the infliction of violence. This is where architecture's pharmacological dimension becomes useful—the more you go into the depths of a poison, the more you can find the possibility of a cure." Eyal Weizman

Yesomi Umolu, "Eyal Weizman and Architecture as Political Intervention,"
in: *Walker Magazine*, September 21, 2012.
http://www.walkerart.org/magazine/2012/eyal-weizman-architecture-confronts-politics

"I am very concerned about positions that conceive of architecture as an instrument of freedom or repression. In fact, I think that the more you want to get into the act of freeing something, the more you need to look into the abyss of the worst architectural possibilities and into the most intense situations of injustice or the infliction of violence. This is where architecture's pharmacological dimension becomes useful—the more you go into the depths of a poison, the more you can find the possibility of a cure." Eyal Weizman

Yasemi Umolu, "Eyal Weizman and Architecture as Political Intervention," in Walker Magazine, September 21, 2012. http://www.walkerart.org/magazine/2012/eyal-weizman-architecture-confronts-politics

BEHIND THE WALL

SHADOWS OF REALITY SHARON RAZ

Performance documentation, Hansen House, Jerusalem, 2015

Performance documentation, Hansen House, Jerusalem, 2015

"And houses get murdered just as their residents get murdered. And as the memory of things get murdered—wood, stone, glass, iron, cement—they all scatter in fragments like beings. And cotton, silk, linen, notepads, books, all are torn like words whose owners were not given time to speak.", Mahmoud Darwish

"The House Murdered," in Progressive, November 2006, Vol. 70, Issue 11, p. 40. http://www.progressive.org/mag/darwishpoem.html

"And houses get murdered just as their residents get murdered. And as the memory of things get murdered—wood, stone, glass, iron, cement—they all scatter in fragments like beings. And cotton, silk, linen, notepads, books, all are torn like words whose owners were not given time to speak." Mahmoud Darwish

"The House Murdered," in: Progressive, November 2006, Vol. 70, Issue 11, p. 40.
http://www.progressive.org/mag/darwishpoem.html

BEHIND THE WALL, 2015
VIDEO, PERFORMANCE
Two channel HD video
11:00 min

Video and performance record experimentally the visualization of real and imaginary borders and segregation. A landscape panorama with various walls and fences shows actors trying to communicate and interact with one another, while others go about their business as if they did not exist. The film images are projected onto a series of tables lying on their side. Although they would be easy to overcome, the performers remain in the limited space behind the tables. Only occasionally are they tempted to intervene in the filmic events across the wall with minimal gestures. The tug-of-war of a group of people in the film marks a half-heartedly executed and quickly ended struggle to pull the other party onto one's own side. Against all practical and political reason, exclusion and isolation are continued: the wall in our minds continues to exist.

Experimentell greifen Video und Performance die Visualisierung realer und imaginärer Grenzziehung und Segregation auf. Ein Landschaftspanorama mit unterschiedlichen Mauern und Zäunen zeigt Akteure im Versuch, über die Grenzen hinweg zu kommunizieren und zu interagieren, während andere ihrer Beschäftigung nachgehen, als ob diese nicht existieren würde. Die Filmbilder sind auf eine Reihe von auf der Seite liegenden Tischen gerichtet. Obwohl sie leicht zu überwinden wären, verharren die Performer im begrenzten Raum dahinter. Nur gelegentlich sind sie versucht, über die Mauer hinweg, mit minimalen Gesten in das filmische Geschehen einzugreifen. Das Tauziehen einer Gruppe von Leuten im Film markiert ein nur halbherzig ausgeführtes und schnell beendetes Ringen darum, die andere Partei auf die eigene Seite zu ziehen. Entgegen jeder praktischen und politischen Vernunft werden Abschottung und Ausgrenzung fortgeführt, die Mauer in den Köpfen hat Bestand.

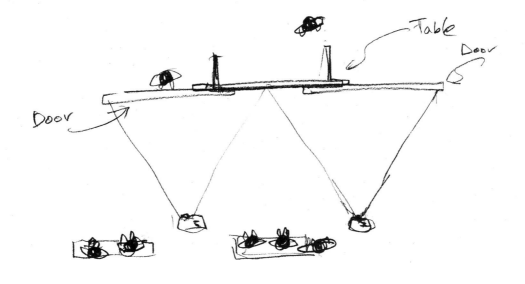

Door

Table

Door

43

WE FORGOT

Performance documentation, FFT Düsseldorf, 2015

Performance documentation, FFT Düsseldorf, 2015

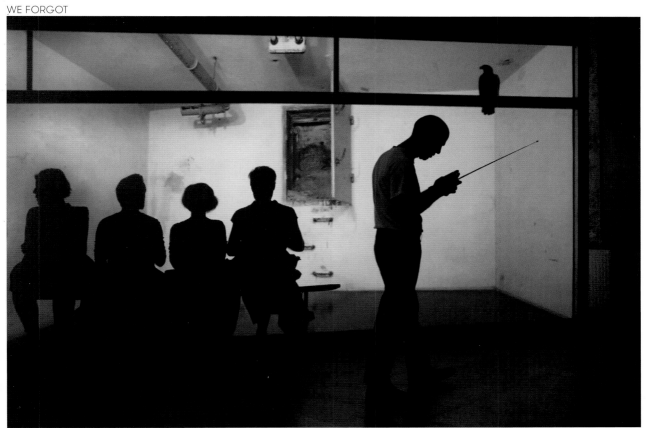

Performance documentation, FFT Düsseldorf, 2015

My Home

Givat Shaul Cemetery, Israel

Jewish Cemetery, Berlin

Bm

"I don't study when people forget. I study the oppsite:

when they remember, when they remember things that

didn't happen or remember things that were different

from the way they really were. I study false memories."

Elisabeth Loftus "How Reliable is Your Memory?," in: *TED Talks*, June 2013.
https://www.ted.com/talks/elizabeth_loftus_the_fiction_of_memory

"I don't study when people forget. I study the oppsite:

when they remember, when they remember things that

didn't happen or remember things that were different

from the way they really were. I study false memories."

Hitler
Blood-stained
suicide sofa
fabric Auction
for $6,000 →

Ambulance, 1962

Summer
2014,
Israel

SHADOWS OF REALLY SHADOW DAZ

WE FORGOT, 2015
VIDEO, PERFORMANCE
Two channel HD video
60:00 min

This video installation and live performance do not represent moments of forgetting as much as they depict processes of the re-construction of individual memory. In the first part, the spectators are invited by performers to explore everyday acts against the backdrop of a video projection. Like the film images themselves, they are dedicated to particular objects such as a broom, a candle, or a shovel. In the second, spatially separated part, the spectators see the slightly modified images showing the interactions of their successors at the same time. A sound track complements the visual narration with personal fragments of memory on war, displacement, and the Holocaust from the perspective of a storyteller. The spectator's achievement of memory is challenged in two ways: the individual's own capacity for memory in relationship to images and acts they have carried out themselves a short while previously, that is, the reconstruction of past from the present, is interrogated at the same time as the "overwriting" of memory with traces of the real or fictive stories of others. Furthermore, the work in various media reminds us that the constitution of memory not only relies on communication and the media, but is also shaped by it.

Videoinstallation und Live Performance repräsentieren weniger Momente des Vergessens als Prozesse der Re-Konstruktion individuellen Erinnerns. Im ersten Teil werden die Zuschauer von Performern eingeladen, vor dem Hintergrund einer Videoprojektion Alltagshandlungen nachzugehen. Diese sind, wie auch die Filmbilder selbst, bestimmten Objekten wie einem Besen, einer Kerze oder einer Schaufel gewidmet. Im zweiten, räumlich getrennten Teil sehen die Zuschauer die leicht modifizierten Bilder, die zugleich die Interaktionen ihrer Nachfolger zeigen. Eine Tonspur ergänzt die visuelle Narration um persönliche Erinnerungsfragmente über Krieg, Vertreibung und den Holocaust aus der Perspektive einer Erzählerin. Die Gedächtnisleistung der Zuschauer wird in zweifacher Hinsicht herausgefordert: Das eigene Erinnerungsvermögen in Bezug auf Bilder und kurz zuvor selbst ausgeführte Handlungen, also die Rekonstruktion von Vergangenheit aus der Gegenwart heraus wird befragt und zugleich das „Überschreiben" von Erinnerung durch die Spuren realer oder fiktiver Geschichten anderer. Darüber hinaus erinnert uns die intermediale Arbeit daran, dass die Konstitution von Erinnerung auf Kommunikation und Medien nicht nur angewiesen, sondern in erster Linie durch sie geprägt ist.

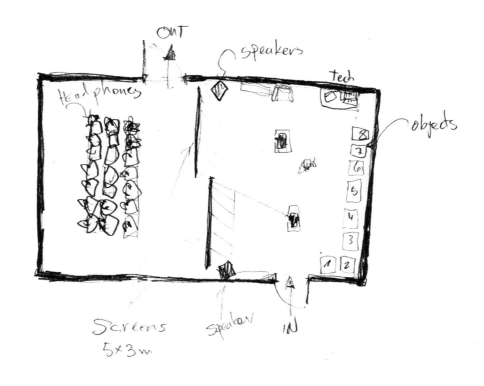

OUT

speakers

tech

Headphones

objects

8
7
6
5
4
3
1 2

Screens
5×3m

speaker

IN

OPEN | CLOSE

SHADOWS OF REALITY SIXTY TWO ROWS 7

Installation view, OKK/Raum29, Berlin, 2014

Installation view, OKK/Raum29, Berlin, 2014

SHADOWS OF REALITY KILWA NUNG

Lions' Gate

"Suleiman built the Lions' Gate to protect Jerusalem from invaders. [...] Israeli paratroops from the 55th Paratroop Brigade came through this gate during the Six-Day War of 1967 and unfurled the Israeli flag above the Temple Mount."

Lions' Gate

"Suleiman built the Lions' Gate to protect Jerusalem
from invaders. [...] Israeli paratroops from the 55th
Paratroop Brigade came through this gate during
the Six-Day War of 1967 and unfurled the Israeli flag
above the Temple Mount."

https://en.wikipedia.org/wiki/Lions'_Gate

1967

Lions Gate,
Jerusalem

OPEN | CLOSE, 2014
VIDEO, PERFORMANCE
Single channel HD video
03:43 min loop

The video deals with borders in their function as political and territorial markings and the violation thereof. Black, gridded shadows at the beginning of the work are revealed to be grilles, doors, and fences placed behind one another. They are slowly pushed to the side with a metallic squeak to reveal the view of a border crossing. Here, a security official examines the bags and passports of those waiting, then allows them to cross. At borders that serve to mark cultural differences, there are different emigration laws depending on nationality, appearance, religious background, and language. By locating the scene specifically at Lions' Gate, one of the many accesses to the fortified old city of Jerusalem, through which trade was carried out, where people arrived in the city, and the Israeli Army passed through in the Six-Day War (1967), the border in the video stands as a synonym for the clash between strategies of security, the experience of a lack of freedom, and enduring armed conflicts.

Das Video beschäftigt sich mit Grenzen in ihrer Funktion als politische sowie territoriale Markierungen und mit deren Überschreiten. Schwarz gerasterte Schatten am Beginn der Arbeit zeigen sich als hintereinander stehende Gitter, Tore und Zäune, die unter metallischem Quietschen nach und nach zur Seite geschoben werden und den Blick auf einen Grenzübergang frei geben. Dort kontrolliert ein Sicherheitsbeamter Taschen und Pässe von Wartenden, um sie anschließend passieren zu lassen. An Grenzen, die der Kennzeichnung kultureller Unterschiede dienen, gelten verschiedene Emigrationsgesetze, abhängig von Nationalität, Aussehen, religiösem Hintergrund und Sprache. Mit der konkreten Verortung der Szene vor dem Löwentor – einem der vielen Zugänge zur befestigten Altstadt Jerusalems –, durch das Handel getrieben wird, Menschen kommen und gehen und durch das die israelische Armee im Sechstagekrieg (1967) gelangte, steht die Grenze im Video als Synonym für das Aufeinandertreffen von Strategien der Sicherheit und der Erfahrung von Unfreiheit sowie für anhaltende bewaffnete Auseinandersetzungen.

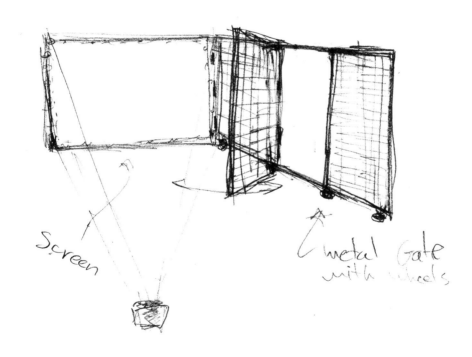

Screen

metal Gate
with wheels

Performance documentation, OKK/Raum29, Berlin, 2014

PARALYZED MOVEMENT

Installation view, Musrara Mix Festival 14, Jerusalem, 2014

AVANT SHAFT SMOTIVA

Installation view, Musrara Mix Festival 14, Jerusalem, 2014

SHADOWS OF REALITY / SHARED IN DR...

PARALYZED MOVEMENT, 2014
VIDEO, PERFORMANCE
Single channel HD video
05:00 min loop

The work installed in public space depicts an absurd scenario. By showing two old soldiers in wheelchairs and their vain attempt at fighting against each other, the video becomes a parable for frozen, unresolved conflicts. The enemies have become paralyzed and are no longer able to approach one another. Except for a temporary uprising linked to scenarios of threat, they have nothing more to say to each other. Despite the realistic background showing a wall and a watchtower, the events become stylistically exaggerated: on the one hand by way of the theatrical performance, and on the other by the two circular frames through which the events can be watched as if through opera glasses. The fighting couple, visually separated and yet intractably linked to each other, is parodied by the interactive play of the shadows of the visitors to the installation, so that the scene acquires a theatrical note.

Die im öffentlichen Raum installierte Arbeit stellt ein absurdes Szenario dar. Indem es zwei alte Soldaten in Rollstühlen und im vergeblichen Versuch zeigt, miteinander zu kämpfen, wird das Video zur Parabel für erstarrte, unlösbare Konflikte. Die Gegner sind bewegungsunfähig geworden und nicht mehr in der Lage, aufeinander zuzugehen. Außer einem temporären Aufbegehren, verbunden mit Drohszenarien, haben sie sich nichts mehr zu sagen. Trotz des realistischen Bildhintergrunds, der eine Mauer und einen Wachturm zeigt, erfährt das Geschehen eine stilistische Überhöhung: Zum einen durch die bühnenartige Inszenierung, zum anderen durch die zwei kreisrunden Bildausschnitte, durch die das Geschehen wie durch ein Theaterglas zu betrachten ist. Das streitende Paar, das visuell getrennt und zugleich unlösbar miteinander verbunden scheint, wird durch interaktive Schattenspiele von Besuchern der Installation parodiert und die Szene theatralisiert.

"Particularly striking is the extent to which all combatants see themselves in terms borrowed from industrial labour. They focus on hitting 'targets' and achieving 'results' as an efficient way of rationalising violence and instrumentalising human casualties." Ben Hutchison

Sönke Neitzel and Harald Welzer, "Soldaten: On Fighting, Killing and Dying," in: *The Guardian*, September 30, 2012.
https://www.theguardian.com/books/2012/sep/30/soldaten-neitzel-welzer-holocaust-review

"Particularly striking is the extent to which all combatants see themselves in terms borrowed from industrial labour. They focus on hitting 'targets' and achieving 'results' as an efficient way of rationalising violence and instrumentalising human casualties." _{Ben Hutchison}

Installation view, Verein zur Förderung von Kunst und Kultur am Rosa-Luxemburg-Platz e.V., Berlin, 2014

Installation view, Verein zur Förderung von Kunst und Kultur am Rosa-Luxemburg-Platz e.V., Berlin, 2014

"Those who do not move, do not notice their chains."

Rosa Luxemburg

"Those who do not move, do not notice their chains."

Rosa Luxemburg

RESTRAINING MOTION, 2014
VIDEO, PERFORMANCE
Two channel HD video
05:00 min loop

Restraining Motion studies the role of the individual in society. The representation of outer constraints and the revolt of the individual are picked up in a stylized choreography. Projected onto the broad façade of windows of a building on Rosa-Luxemburg-Platz in Berlin, the filmic production looks like shadow theater for the audience and random passersby. In linking film and live performance, the work reveals tragic and comic elements. The performers are captured in an absurd work cycle by the repetition of movement. The conceptual starting point for the work lies in the ideas on social justice and pacifism of communist theorist and politician Rosa Luxemburg and her aphorism, "Those who do not move cannot feel their chains."

Restraining Motion untersucht die Rolle des Individuums in der Gesellschaft. Die Repräsentation äußerer Zwänge sowie das Aufbegehren des Einzelnen werden in einer stilisierten Choreographie aufgegriffen. Projiziert auf die breite Fensterfront eines Gebäudes am Rosa-Luxemburg-Platz in Berlin erscheint die filmische Inszenierung sowohl für die Besucher als auch die Passanten als Schattentheater. In der Verknüpfung von Film und Live Performance weist die Arbeit tragische und komische Elemente auf. Die Performer sind durch die andauernde Wiederholung von Bewegungsabläufen in einem absurden Arbeitskreislauf gefangen. Als konzeptioneller Ausgangspunkt der Arbeit gelten die Ideen der kommunistischen Theoretikerin und Politikerin Rosa Luxemburg zu sozialer Gerechtigkeit und Pazifismus wie auch der von ihr stammende Aphorismus: „Wer sich nicht bewegt, spürt seine Fesseln nicht."

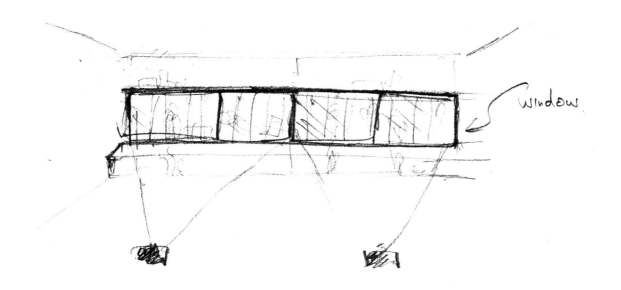

window

THE RIGHT TO LEAVE

SHADOWS OF REALITY SHARON PAZ

Installation view, Verein zur Förderung von Kunst und Kultur am Rosa-Luxemburg-Platz e.V., Berlin, 2014

SHADOWS OF REALITY SPARON PAY

THE RIGHT TO LEAVE, 2013
VIDEO, PERFORMANCE
Single channel HD video
04:00 min loop

Thematically speaking, the work deals with processes of migration. A train, which consists of a so-called mobile "Raumerweiterungshalle" or "Room Expansion Hall" (REH) made in the GDR, leads past snowy forests and desert landscapes, then stops again at the point of departure surrounded by a barbed wire fence. Inside, the inmates play the well-known children's game *Musical Chairs*. The principle of free migration, the right to leave and to seek a country of one's own choosing, is here represented in contrary dynamics. Global freedom of movement is represented in the video as limited by borders and as a cycle of emigration and forced return that is difficult to break. Open immigration as a human right is only available to the few who are chosen in the selection process. The chairs of the projection invite the beholders to become a shadowy part of the endless traveling and returning.

Thematisch befasst sich die Arbeit mit Migrationsprozessen. Ein Zug, dessen Waggons aus der in der DDR gefertigten, transportablen Raumerweiterungshalle (REH) bestehen, fährt an verschneiten Wäldern und Wüstenlandschaften vorbei, um wieder am von Stacheldrahtzaun umgebenen Ausgangspunkt zu halten. Im Inneren spielen die Insassen das bekannte Kinderspiel *Reise nach Jerusalem*. Das Prinzip der freien Migration, das Recht zu gehen und ein Land der eigenen Wahl aufzusuchen, wird hier in gegenläufiger Dynamik dargestellt. Globale Bewegungsfreiheit repräsentiert sich im Video als durch Grenzen eingeschränkt und als ein nicht zu durchbrechender Kreislauf von Auswanderung und erzwungener Rückkehr. Offene Einwanderung als Menschenrecht steht nur Auserwählten zu, die durch Selektionsverfahren bestimmt werden. Die Stuhlreihe vor der Videoprojektion lädt die Betrachter ein, schattenhafter Teil der endlosen Reise und Wiederkehr zu werden.

Reise nach Jerusalem

(Musical Chairs/Journey to Jerusalem)

"The origin of the name is unclear. Some people
suspect it refers to traveling to Jerusalem at the time
of the Crusades, which resulted in such tremendous
losses for the peoples of Europe; others suspect
the origin lies in the time of the Zionist migration
to Palestine and the limited space available on the
emigrant ships."

http://memim.com/musical-chairs.html

Reise nach Jerusalem.

(Musical Chairs/Journey to Jerusalem)

"The origin of the name is unclear. Some people suspect it refers to traveling to Jerusalem at the time of the Crusades, which resulted in such tremendous losses for the peoples of Europe; others suspect the origin lies in the time of the Zionist migration to Palestine and the limited space available on the emigrant ships.".

REH
Raumerweiterungshalle =
Space-extending building

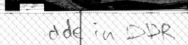
dde in DDR

SHADED WINDOWS

Performance documentation, Pavillon am Milchhof, Berlin, 2012

Performance documentation, Pavillon am Milchhof, Berlin, 2012

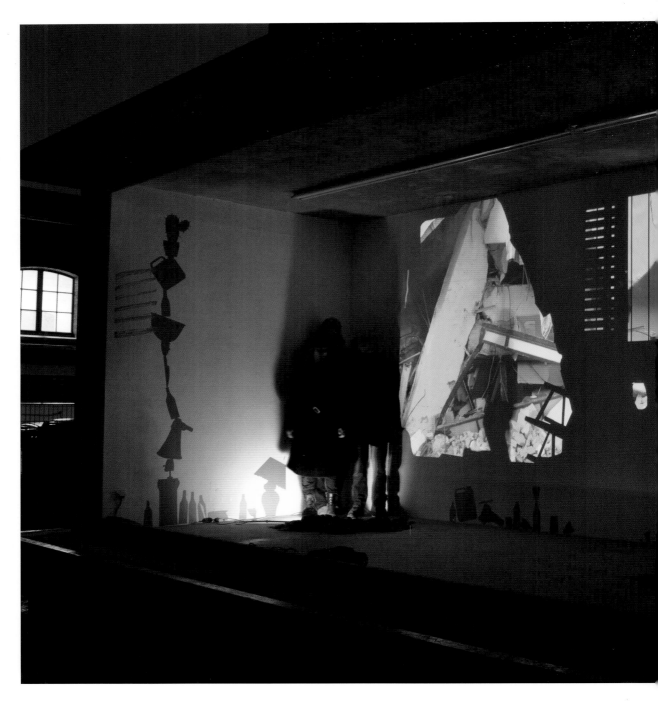

Performance documentation, Pavillon am Milchhof, Berlin, 2012

He broke the wall, testimony catalog number: 120033, rank: Staff Sergeant, unit: Engineering Corps, area: Nablus area, period: August 2002.

"Most of my work was on arrest missions, but there were also ongoing actions. I can seriously say that those were the most problematic. I happened to enter Nablus three times. This was in August 2002. We began searches on a street called 'Jacob's Ladder', inside the Casbah. Mostly we moved through walls."

— How was this done?

"With hammers and so on. There I can really attest to one of the exceptions [...] of abusing civilian population. There was a case where we had the Palestinian home-owner break his own wall. It was a really big wall, and the whole force went through."

"Israeli Soldiers Talk about the Occupied Territories", in: Breaking the Silence.
http://www.breakingthesilence.org.il/

He broke the wall, testimony catalog number: 120033, rank: Staff Sergeant, unit: Engineering Corps, area: Nablus area, period: August 2002

"Most of my work was on arrest missions, but there were also ongoing actions. I can seriously say that those were the most problematic. I happened to enter Nablus three times. This was in August 2002. We began searches on a street called 'Jacob's Ladder', inside the Casbah. Mostly we moved through walls."

— *How was this done?*

"With hammers and so on. There I can really attest to one of the exceptions [...] of abusing civilian population. There was a case where we had the Palestinian home- owner break his own wall. It was a really big wall, and the whole force went through."

"Israeli Soldiers Talk about the Occupied Territories," in: *Breaking the Silence*.
http://www.breakingthesilence.org.il/

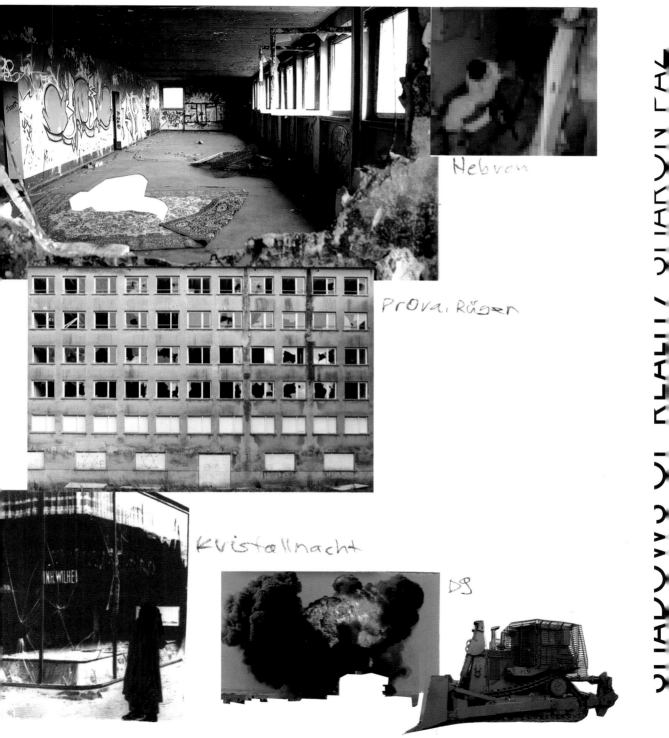

Hebron

Prora, Rügen

Kristallnacht

D9

SHADED WINDOWS, 2012
VIDEO, PERFORMANCE
Two channel HD video
17:45 min

The thematic layer of the video installation and site-specific performance tells of initially peaceful everyday scenes in the private sphere of a residential building, where devastating acts of violent conflict are announced and then take place. The real space of performance undergoes a similar change. As a site of protection and intimacy, it undergoes a violent transformation in destroyed habitats and living space. Its residents experience the exclusion from their own home and its final loss. In that the shadows of the performers overlap with the schematic figures of videos, the events are multiplied and distorted at the same time. The glass pavilion can be entered as a site of performance and provides the best possible transparency and changing perspectives both inside and outside. The events in the video in contrast, the outlooks and views inside the various spaces, are fragmented by blinds, walls, and other barriers. In particular the motif of the blind as protecting from view runs as a film-analytic commentary through the entire video. Like the opening and closing of a photographic aperture, it lends certain events clear visibility and focus, while it moves others out of focus and only allows them to be seen in part. Metaphorically speaking, the work refers to the tension between the refusal and the expansion of the gaze.

Die inhaltliche Ebene der Videoinstallation und ortsspezifischen Performance erzählt von zunächst friedlichen Alltagsszenen in der Privatsphäre eines Wohnhauses, in denen sich verheerende Akte von kriegerischen Konflikten ankündigen und schließlich vollziehen. Der reale Raum der Aufführung durchläuft eine ähnliche Veränderung. Als Ort des Schutzes und der Intimität erfährt er eine gewaltsame Umwandlung in zerstörten Lebens- und Wohnraum. Seine Bewohner erleben den Ausschluss aus dem eigenen Zuhause und seinen endgültigen Verlust. Indem die Schatten der Performer die schemenhaften Figuren des Videos überlagern, vervielfältigt und verzerrt sich zugleich das Geschehen. Der Glaspavillon als Aufführungsort ist begehbar und sorgt von Innen und Außen für größtmögliche Transparenz und wechselnde Perspektiven. Die Vorkommnisse im Video hingegen, die Aus- und Einblicke in verschiedene Räume, werden durch Jalousien, Mauern und andere Barrieren fragmentiert. Insbesondere das Motiv der Jalousie als Sichtschutz zieht sich als filmanalytischer Kommentar durch das Video. Gleich den sich öffnenden und schließenden Lamellen einer fotografischen Blende verleiht sie bestimmten Ereignissen deutliche Sichtbarkeit und Schärfe, während sie andere aus dem Fokus rückt und nur lückenhaft zu sehen gibt. Metaphorisch verweist die Arbeit auf die Gegensatzspannung zwischen Verweigerung und Erweiterung des Blicks.

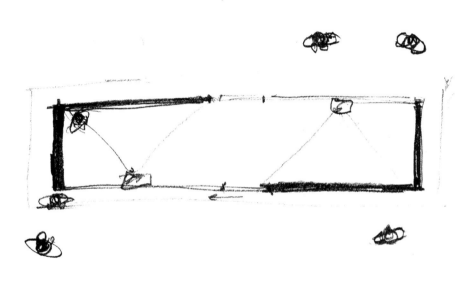

JO WALLS

Installation view, Bernauer Straße, U8 subway station, Berlin, 2013

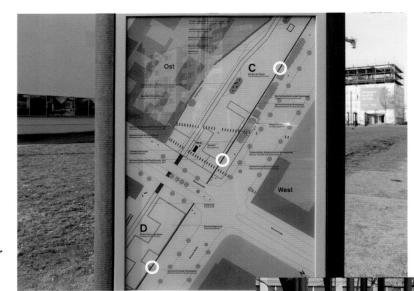

Bernauer Str.
Wall memorial

West

"For more than an hour, Leibing stood watching the nervous young non-commissioned officer as he paced back and forth, his PPSh-41 slung over his shoulder, smoking one cigarette after another. 'Come on over, come on over!' (Komm' rüber!) the West Berlin crowd on Bernauer Strasse chanted. 'He's going to jump!' one passerby remarked. And at four p.m. on August 15, 1961, Leibing got lucky. Schumann tossed aside his cigarette, then turned and ran for the coil of barbed wire that marked the boundary between East and West. He jumped, flinging away his gun as he flew, and Leibing clicked the shutter […]."

"Conrad Schumann defects to West Berlin, 1961," in: *Rare Historical Photos*, July 17, 2014.
http://rarehistoricalphotos.com/conrad-schumann-defects-west-berlin-1961/

"For more than an hour, Leibing stood watching the nervous young non-commissioned officer as he paced back and forth, his PPSh-41 slung over his shoulder, smoking one cigarette after another. 'Come on over, come on over!' (Komm, rüber!) the West Berlin crowd on Bernauer Strasse chanted. 'He's going to jump!', one passerby remarked. And at four p.m. on August 15, 1961, Leibing got lucky. Schumann tossed aside his cigarette, then turned and ran for the coil of barbed wire that marked the boundary between East and West. He jumped, flinging away his gun as he flew, and Leibing clicked the shutter [...].".

"Conrad Schumann defects to West Berlin, 1961," in Rare Historical Photos, July 17, 2014,
http://rarehistoricalphotos.com/conrad-schumann-defects-west-berlin-1961/

Bernauer Straße

1961

East

NO WALLS, 2013
Six posters
each 252 x 356 cm

The installation of black-and-white posters in the subway station at Bernauer Straße refers directly to the history of the location. During the Cold War and until the 1980s the house façades along this street in the divided Berlin represented part of the Berlin Wall separating East from West Berlin. Here, captured in photographs and films, dramatic scenes of escape from windows and through tunnels played out. Today, the station is the starting point for many tourists visiting the monument. Current shots of both sides of Bernauer Straße are combined on the large-format posters with scenes from historical photographs in which people are visible as mere shadows in flight, at demonstrations, or in the attempt to communicate across the border. Although the fall of the Wall marked the end of the Cold War and was considered a symbol of hope for the tearing down of other borders, the past lies like a dark shadow on the present, where the renewal of nationalist isolation and the erection of political borders is currently playing out around the world.

Die Installation schwarz-weißer Plakatwände in der U-Bahn-Station Bernauer Straße verweist unmittelbar auf die Geschichte des Ortes. Im geteilten Berlin zu Zeiten des Kalten Krieges bildeten bis in die 1980er-Jahre die Hausfassaden entlang der Straße einen Teil der Berliner Mauer, die Ost- und Westberlin voneinander trennte. Hier spielten sich – bis heute durch Fotografien und Filme vermittelt – dramatische Szenen der Flucht aus Fenstern und durch selbst gegrabene Tunnel ab. Heute ist die Station Ausgangspunkt zahlreicher Touristen für den Besuch der Gedenkstätte. Aktuelle Aufnahmen von beiden Seiten der Bernauer Straße sind auf den großformatigen Plakaten kombiniert mit Szenen historischer Fotografien, in denen Menschen auf der Flucht, bei Demonstrationen oder dem Versuch der Verständigung über die Grenze hinweg – hier nur noch in schattenhafter Existenz – zu sehen sind. Obwohl der Mauerfall das Ende des Kalten Krieges markierte und als Hoffnungssymbol für das Niederreißen anderer Staatsgrenzen galt, legt sich die Vergangenheit wie ein dunkler Widerschein auf die Gegenwart, in der sich ihrerseits die Erneuerung nationalistischer Abschottung und das Errichten politischer Grenzen weltweit abspielt.

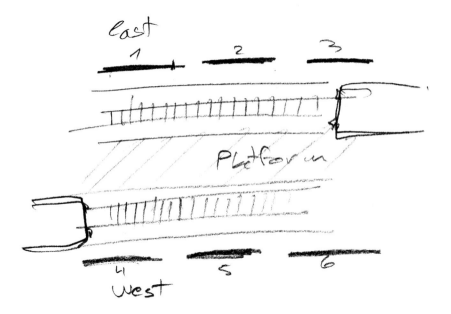

east

1   2   3

Platform

4   5   6

West

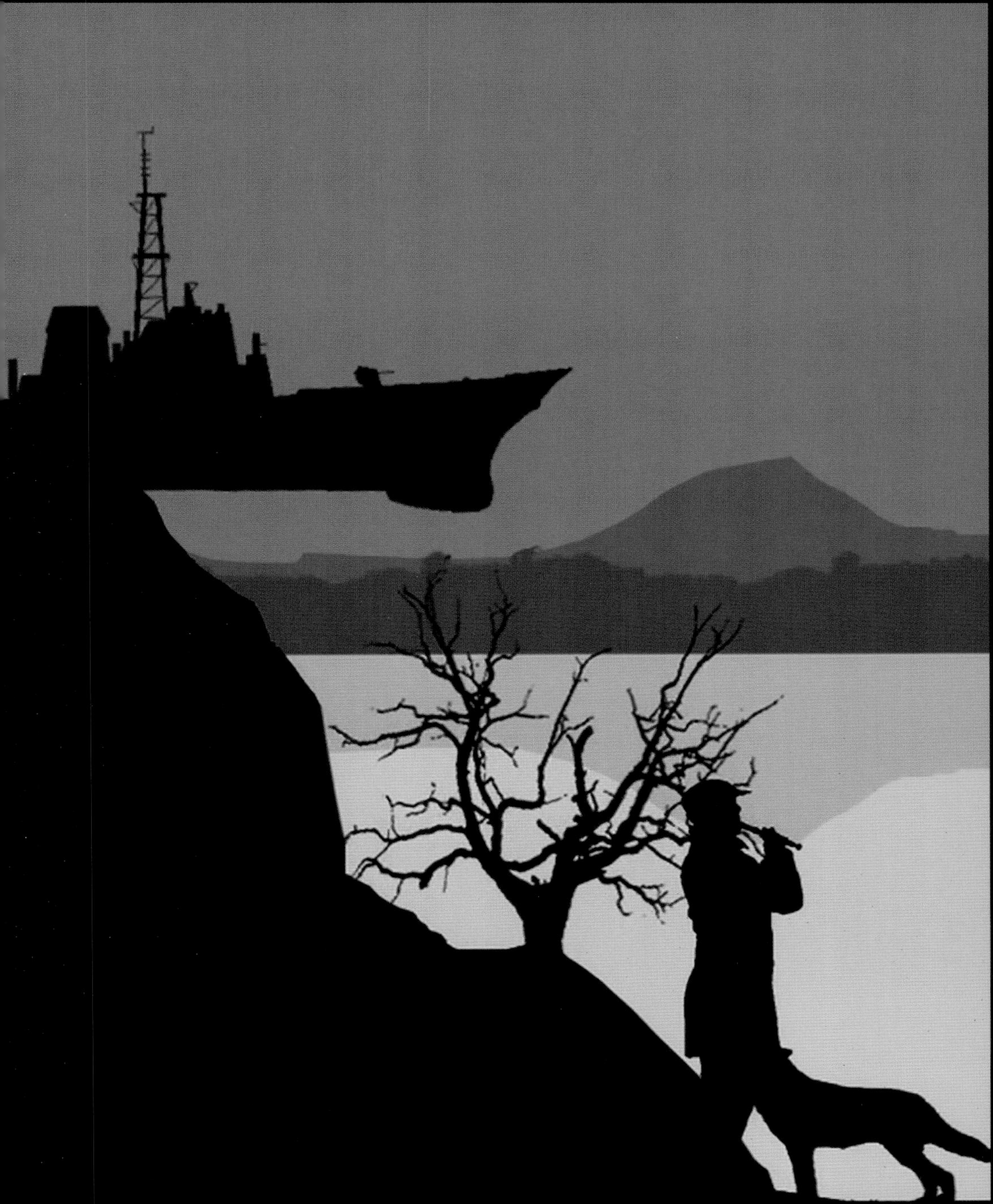

THE KING IS BLIND

Performance documentation, Hafen Hildesheim, 2011

Siegessäule

"Power corresponds to the human ability not just to act but to act in concert. Power is never the property of an individual; it belongs to a group and remains in existence only so long as the group keeps together. When we say of somebody that he is 'in power,' we actually refer to his being empowered by a certain number of people to act in their name." Hannah Arendt

On Violence, San Diego 1969, p. 44.

"Power corresponds to the human ability not just to act but to act in concert. Power is never the property of an individual; it belongs to a group and remains in existence only so long as the group keeps together. When we say of somebody that he is 'in power' we actually refer to his being empowered by a certain number of people to act in their name." Hannah Arendt

On Violence, San Diego 1969, p. 44.

The Aral Spring

THE KING IS BLIND, 2011
VIDEO, PERFORMANCE
Single channel HD video
22:00 min

Using the historical figure of the king as the sovereign of the state, the work explores the dynamics of the abuse of power, subjection, and violence. The combination of video projection and performance, human silhouettes in two-dimensional, animated surroundings, and the shadows of the live performers before and behind the screen results in a collage of a number of historical and current events and sites. Military conflicts and other traumatic events are evoked that are linked to one another by the appearance of the monarchic despot and his subjects. The final scene shows the blind king on a representative memorial column, removed from real events by self-aggrandizement, and finally the replacement of the vacant space with a new ruler.

Anhand der historischen Figur des Königs als höchstem Souverän des Staates spürt die Arbeit den Dynamiken von Machtmissbrauch, Unterwerfung und Gewalt nach. Die Kombination von Videoprojektion und Performance, menschlichen Silhouetten in zweidimensionaler, animierter Umgebung und den Schatten der Live Performer vor sowie hinter der Leinwand ergeben eine Collage aus zahlreichen historischen und aktuellen Ereignissen wie Schauplätzen. Kriegerische Auseinandersetzungen und andere traumatische Geschehnisse werden aufgerufen, die durch das Erscheinen des monarchischen Despoten und seiner Untertanen miteinander verknüpft werden. Die Schlussszene zeigt den blinden König auf einer repräsentativen Ehrensäule, den realen Ereignissen durch Selbstherrlichkeit enthoben und schließlich erstarrt zum monumentalen Denkmal. Sein späteres Verschwinden antizipiert bereits die Neubesetzung des leer gewordenen Platzes durch einen nachfolgenden Herrscher.

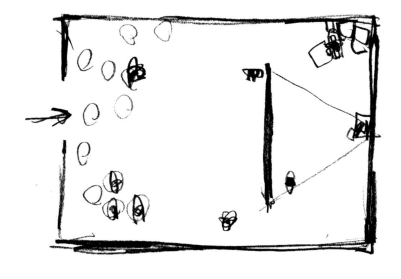

Ines Lindner

Between Image and Projection
The Performance-Based Video Works of Sharon Paz

In her work, Sharon Paz explores power relations and their consequences. They can be coagulated as an architecture or a landscape, or can become palpable in small scenes. The actors themselves remain invisible; only their shadows emerge before the filmed backdrop. Figures and actions are typified. Their choreography is superimposed onto the video image.

Usually, the silhouettes are part of the video work projected in the exhibition space. Sometimes they are generated by a live performance: the actors perform in the space between the projector and the projection surface. The exhibition visitors can inspect this intermediate space. It thus becomes clear that the shadows do not precisely overlap with the image. The bodies of the actors interrupt the projection beam. Usually in a projection the bundled light passes through a space kept free of disturbance in order to transfer the visual information. In Paz, this apparently neutral space between the image and the reproduction of the image is actively occupied. Here, the space between image and projection that is blocked out in standard forms of image perception becomes a space of action. The beholder can also pass through this intermediate space and his or her shadow—intentionally or unintentionally—can become part of the work for a moment.

As complex as Paz's works might be in terms of structure, they are equally clear in their appearance. In the one-channel installation *Open / Close* (2014), the shadows of gates and fences close back and forth, squeaking and grinding. Shadow figures rush back and forth, wait or lash out at one another. The original black gradually lightens and a door becomes visible. The work seems to be a generally human parable on the blocked access and the unrest and aggression that it can trigger. The gate is not just any gate, but Jerusalem's Lions' Gate, which leads into the Old City in the Muslim Quarter.

Paz was born in Israel and lives in Berlin. Her works refer frequently to concrete political relations. They deal with Israeli policy and German history, with trauma, memory, and forgetting. The scenes that Paz develops for her works are condensations that both intensify experience and keep their distance from concrete events.

This is also true of her use of sound. It always has a clear reference to the event being alluded to, but is a bit more complicated than a sound that merely accompanies the images. It seems typified. In a similar way, she uses the abstract impact of shadow. The reduction awakens our imaginative powers. We immediately begin to interpret the figures. It is rather like when we make shadows of bunnies on the wall with two fingers stretched out from our fist. The space between hand and shadow becomes a space of transformation in which the given is reduced and can be transformed to the imagined.

According to the myth of the emergence of the art of drawing, a woman is said to have captured the outlines of her lover before he went off to war.[1] This legend combines the shadow with absence, death, and longing as the beginning of the art of drawing and providing a sign. On the one hand rudimentary, on the other fantastic. Both have accompanied the shadow play in various cultures. Silhouettes are used for the Javanese theater of gods and heroes. In the salons of the 18th century, producing silhouettes was a popular pastime. In her art, Kara Walker has recourse to silhouettes in American folk art for her panoramas of slave history. William Kentridge uses them in his recent video works to narrate the oppression of blacks in South Africa. The link between black silhouettes and the representation of oppression and racism has a hint of self-evidence to it. In the works of both artists, the black figures stand out from a bright, neutral backdrop. This corresponds to the tradition of the silhouette. Paz, in contrast, uses video images. She creates a media layering that sets the stylized shadows in tension with the depiction of concrete locations.

In the work *We Forgot* (2015), the spectators can look into the space in which the shadows are created and can follow the actions of the performers. In a live performance, the status of the media projection changes. It stops appearing as a simulated present. The video images are past, dream, and imagination. The performance, however, takes place here and now.

The classic form of combining projection and live performance can still be found today at Prague's Laterna Magika.[2] The variety-show effect consists in calibrating the body movements of the actors perfectly to match the space of illusion of the film and both fuse in the perception of the spectators. But the entertainment factor lies in the fact that the spectator never forgets that the apparent naturalness of impression results from the often near-acrobatic efforts of the actors to synchronize their movement with the projected images. Sometimes, Paz plays with the congruency of projection and performance, but usually it is about the difference.

The performance projection *We Forgot* includes the spectator. A group is given instructions that a second group, which has been watching, then repeats. It is the same and yet not the same. As in retelling a tale, the repetition brings the action up to date. The action, its repetition, and the memory of the action are never brought into sync. The play with difference allows for a creative space of perception and composition, but at the same time is also the source of doubt and conflict. Was it this way? Or different? Who decides this? What consequences result from the difference?

In Paz's works, it is often about the reflective distance, a space of thought and imagination that helps to change the view of conflict situations. When Paz superimposes the shadow play of two fighting individuals in wheelchairs onto ruins (*Paralyzed Movement*, 2014), the entire absurdity of the violent conflict is made visible. In another work she takes up the difficult subject of exile in a simple and poetic way (*The Right to Leave*, 2013). Through the windows of passing rail cars, we can see Israeli landscapes and views of the Black Forest. The schematic outlines of the rail cars can be traced back to the silhouette of the *Raumerweiterungshalle*, or literally "space expansion hall," a foldable and easily transportable pavilion that was developed in East Germany to provide extra room whenever needed. Another sequence of the work is about the lack of room. In the game *Musical Chairs* there is always one chair fewer than the number of participants in the game. They run around the line of empty chairs while the music plays. Whenever it suddenly stops, each player tries to sit on a chair. One player will always remain standing and is then excluded from the game. Researchers attribute the German name of the game, *Reise nach Jerusalem*, or *Journey to Jerusalem*, to the fact that room on the journey to the Promised Land was always limited. In Paz's work, it could also allude to the dramatic conditions of those driven into exile by German Fascism. The title *The Right to Leave* is perhaps a reference to the fact that Israelis are now taking advantage of their right to take the reverse route and withdraw from their national "duty" to remain. Finding a place here can depend on the moment in history in question.

In developing her works the artist refers repeatedly to the conditions in both countries. *No Walls* (2013) reflects on the German division and was on view at Bernauer Strasse subway station. Paz presented the two-channel installation *Blind Spots* (2016) at KulturRaum in the Zwingli-Kirche, located in Berlin-Friedrichshain. One of the projections filled the side wall of an ascending stairwell and showed silhouettes of figures digging in the soil. The upper part of the projection was thrown onto the wall behind it. It was beamed step by step onto the rear wall of the stairwell, as if things were placed there. Those who went up or down the stairs became part of the work with their shadow and walked through the scenes of digging. Was a tunnel being dug out? Was this an act of excavation or perhaps burial? The ambivalence is characteristic for the poetic and parable-like aspect of Paz's works, which often have a tendency towards the absurd. Alongside the stair projection there is a second, smaller projection that beams a hole in the wall just over the floor. Very frequently, Paz's video images lead across a threshold to a different place. Windows, doors, holes, and tunnels set limits and open passages. The usually dark framing outlines them and emphasizes the transition from one realm to the next. Not everything is visible. The framing concentrates the gaze, stimulating our curiosity to see what remains hidden to us.

When the stairs are climbed upstairs, such a site of transition is revealed. Those who looked carefully could discover that the second video showed the very corridor into which one could look. The miniaturized repetition showed simply what could be seen above, and yet it seemed different, more secret.

Paz also directs our attention at the space between the image and the reproduction of the image when she is not using a choreography

of shadows. And yet, the movement of shadows makes the otherwise neutral space available to experience as a space of action. In that the actors interrupt the projection beam with their bodies, it becomes a space of transformation. On the projection surface, this interruption seems like a media layering. Film image and shadow play are related to each other. But because they belong to two different levels of representation, they remain separate for the beholder. The difference opens a space that refers to the real space between image and projection, which can be used for reflections and interventions.

[1] Pliny the Elder, "The Inventors of the Art of Modelling," in: *The Natural History*, Book XXXV, Chap. 43, ed. by John Bostock and H.T. Riley, London 1855.
[2] Alfréd Radok developed the first program as the Czechoslovakian contribution to Expo 1958 in Brussels.

Ines Lindner

Zwischen Bild und Projektion
Zu den performancebasierten Videoarbeiten von
Sharon Paz

Sharon Paz setzt sich in ihren Arbeiten mit
Machtverhältnissen und ihren Folgen ausei-
nander. Sie können in einer Architektur oder
Landschaft geronnen sein oder werden durch
kleine Szenen greifbar. Die Akteure selbst bleiben
unsichtbar, nur ihre Schatten schieben sich vor
den gefilmten Hintergrund. Figuren und Aktionen
wirken typisiert. Ihre Choreographie überlagert
das Videobild.

   Meistens sind die Silhouetten bereits Teil der
im Ausstellungsraum projizierten Videoarbeit.
Manchmal werden sie durch eine Live Performance erzeugt: Die Handelnden agieren im
Raum zwischen dem Projektor und der Projektionsfläche. Dieser Zwischenraum ist für die
Ausstellungsbesucher einsehbar. Dabei wird
deutlich, dass genau genommen die Schatten
nicht das Bild überlagern. Die Körper der Akteure
unterbrechen den Projektionsstrahl. Normaler-
weise durchquert das gebündelte Licht einen
störungsfrei gehaltenen Raum, um die Bildin-
formation zu übertragen. Bei Paz wird dieser

scheinbar neutrale Raum zwischen Bild und Bildwiedergabe aktiv besetzt. Der in der Bildwahrnehmung ausgeblendete Raum zwischen Bild und Projektion wird zum Handlungsraum. Auch der Betrachter kann diesen Zwischenraum durchqueren und mit seinem Schatten – beabsichtigt oder unbeabsichtigt – für einen Moment Teil der Arbeit werden.

So komplex Paz' Arbeiten der Struktur nach sind, so klar sind sie in ihrer Erscheinung. In der Ein-Kanal-Installation *Open | Close* (2014) schieben sich die Schatten von Toren, Zäunen und Gattern knirschend und ächzend zurück. Schattenfiguren eilen hin und her, warten oder werden handgreiflich. Die anfängliche Schwärze lichtet sich Zug um Zug, und ein Tor wird sichtbar. Die Arbeit scheint eine allgemein menschliche Parabel über versperrte Zugänge zu sein und über die Unruhe und Aggression, die dadurch ausgelöst werden. Das Tor ist aber nicht irgendein Tor, sondern das Löwentor in Jerusalem, das in das muslimische Viertel der Altstadt führt.

Paz ist in Israel geboren und lebt in Berlin. Ihre Arbeiten beziehen sich häufig auf konkrete politische Verhältnisse. Sie haben mit israelischer Politik zu tun und deutscher Geschichte, mit Trauma, Erinnerung und Vergessen. Die Szenen, die Paz für ihre Arbeiten entwickelt, sind Verdichtungen, die Erfahrungen zugleich intensivieren und Abstand zu konkreten Ereignissen halten.

Das gilt auch für den Ton, den sie einsetzt. Er hat immer eine klare Referenz zum angedeuteten Geschehen, ist aber gewissermassen kompakter als ein bloß begleitendes Geräusch. Es wirkt typisiert. Ähnlich setzt sie die abstrahierende Wirkung der Schatten ein. Die Reduktion weckt unsere Vorstellungskraft. Wir fangen sofort an, die Figuren zu deuten. Ein bisschen ist es, wie mit dem Hasen auf der Wand, den wir mit zwei gestreckten Fingern aus der Faust machen: Der Raum zwischen Hand und Schatten wird zu einem Transformationsraum, in dem Gegebenes reduziert wird und sich in Imaginiertes verwandeln kann.

Der Mythos von der Entstehung der Zeichenkunst will, dass eine Frau den Schattenriss ihres Geliebten beim Abschied festhielt, bevor er in den Krieg zog.[1] Diese Überlieferung verbindet den Schatten mit Abwesenheit, Tod und Begehren als Beginn der Zeichenkunst und des Zeichengebens: Einerseits rudimentär, andererseits fantastisch. Beides begleitet das Schattenspiel durch die Kulturen. Scherenschnitt wird für das Javanische Bühnenspiel von Göttern und Helden benutzt. In den Salons des 18. Jahrhunderts dient er zum Zeitvertreib. Die Künstlerin Kara Walker greift auf die in den USA volkstümlich gewordenen Scherenschnitte für ihre Panoramen zur Sklavengeschichte zurück. William Kentridge setzt sie in neueren Videoarbeiten ein, um von der Unterdrückung der Schwarzen in Südafrika zu erzählen. Die Verbindung zwischen den schwarzen Silhouetten und der Darstellung von Unterdrückung und Rassismus hat eine gewisse Evidenz. Bei beiden Künstlern heben sich die schwarzen Figuren von einem hellen, neutralen Grund ab. Das entspricht der Tradition des Scherenschnitts. Paz dagegen nutzt Videobilder. Sie erzeugt eine mediale Schichtung, die die Schattenstilisierung zur Wiedergabe konkreter Orte in Spannung setzt.

In der Arbeit *We Forgot* (2015) können die Zuschauer den Raum, in dem die Schatten erzeugt werden, einsehen und die Aktionen der Performer verfolgen. Bei einer Live Performance ändert sich der Status der medialen Projektion. Sie hört auf, als simulierte Gegenwart zu wirken. Die Videobilder sind Vergangenheit, Traum, Imagination. Die Performance aber findet hier und jetzt statt.

Die klassische Form der Verbindung von Projektion und Live Performance hat bis heute in der Laterna Magika in Prag einen Ort.[2] Der Varieté-Effekt besteht darin, dass die Körperbewegungen der Akteure perfekt auf den Illusionsraum des Films abgestimmt sind und beide in der Wahrnehmung des Zuschauers verschmelzen. Der Unterhaltungswert besteht darin, dass er keinen Moment vergisst, dass die scheinbare Natürlichkeit des Eindrucks sich der oft akrobatischen Anstrengung der Akteure verdankt, ihre Bewegung mit den projizierten Bildern zu synchronisieren. Manchmal spielt Paz mit der Kongruenz von Projektion und Performance, aber meistens geht es visuell um die Differenz.

Die Performance-Projektion *We Forgot* bezieht die Zuschauer ein. Eine Gruppe bekommt Handlungsanweisungen, die eine zweite, die zugeschaut hat, wiederholt. Es ist dasselbe und doch nicht dasselbe. Wie in der Überlieferung wird durch Wiederholung aktualisiert. Die Aktion, ihre Wiederholung und die Erinnerung an die Aktion werden nie zur Deckung kommen. Das Spiel der Differenz ermöglicht einen kreativen Wahrnehmungs- und Gestaltungsraum – aber zugleich ist es auch der Quellgrund von Zweifel und Konflikt. War es so? War es anders?

Wer bestimmt das? Welche Folgen können sich aus der Differenz ergeben?

In Paz' Arbeiten geht es um die reflexive Distanz, einen Denk- und Vorstellungsraum, der hilft, den Blick auf Konfliktsituationen zu ändern. Wenn Paz Ruinen durch ein Schattenspiel von sich prügelnden Rollstuhlfahrern überlagert (*Paralyzed Movement*, 2014), wird die ganze Absurdität des Gewaltkonflikts sichtbar. In einer anderen Arbeit greift sie das so schwierige Thema des Exils in einer ebenso einfachen wie poetischen Weise auf (*The Right to Leave*, 2013). Durch die Fenster vorbeiziehender Wagons sieht man sowohl israelische Landschaften als auch Ansichten des Schwarzwalds. Der schattenhafte Umriss der Wagen geht auf die Silhouette einer Raumerweiterungshalle zurück. Die zusammenfaltbare und leicht zu transportierende Pavillonarchitektur wurde in der DDR entwickelt, um überall zusätzlich Platz schaffen zu können. In einer anderen Sequenz der Arbeit geht es um Platzmangel. Das Spiel *Reise nach Jerusalem* basiert darauf, dass es immer einen Stuhl weniger gibt als Teilnehmer am Spiel. Sie laufen um die aufgereihten, leeren Stühle herum, während eine Musik spielt. Wenn sie unvorhersehbar und abrupt aufhört, versuchen alle einen Sitzplatz zu ergattern. Ein Spieler wird immer übrig bleiben und ausgeschlossen vom Spiel. Forscher führen die deutsche Bezeichnung *Reise nach Jerusalem* darauf zurück, dass die Plätze für die Überfahrt ins gelobte Land schon immer knapp waren. Bei Paz könnte es auch auf die dramatischen Bedingungen der vom deutschen Faschismus ins Exil Getriebenen anspielen. Das Recht zu gehen, wie es im Titel heisst, ist vielleicht eine Anspielung darauf, dass Israelis heute das Recht in Anspruch nehmen, den umgekehrten Weg einzuschlagen und sich der nationalen ‚Pflicht' zu bleiben, entziehen. Einen Platz zu finden kann hier wie da vom gegebenen Moment in der Geschichte abhängen.

Die Künstlerin bezieht sich immer wieder auf die Verhältnisse in beiden Ländern, um ihre Arbeiten zu entwickeln. *No Walls* (2013) reflektiert die deutsche Teilung und war in der U-Bahn-Station Bernauer Strasse zu sehen. Die 2-Kanal-Installation *Blind Spots* (2016) zeigte Sharon Paz im KulturRaum Zwingli-Kirche in Berlin-Friedrichshain. Eine der Projektionen füllte die gemauerte Seitenwand einer aufsteigenden Treppe. Silhouetten grabender Figuren wühlten sich dort in die Erde. Der obere Teil der Projektion lag auf der Wand dahinter. Sie beamte Stufe für Stufe Stapel auf die Rückwand der Treppe, als wären dort Sachen abgelegt. Wer auf- oder abstieg, wurde mit seinem Schatten Teil der Arbeit und schritt dabei über die Szenen des Grabens hinweg. Wird da ein Tunnel ausgehoben? Handelt es sich um eine Aktion des Freilegens oder vielleicht des Vergrabens? Die Mehrdeutigkeit ist charakteristisch für das Poetische und Parabelhafte von Paz' Arbeiten, die häufig eine leichte Neigung zum Absurden zeigen. Seitlich zu der Treppenprojektion gab es eine zweite, kleinere Projektion, die ein Mauerloch knapp über dem Boden an die Wand beamte. Sehr häufig führen uns Paz' Videobilder an eine Schwelle zu einem anderen Ort. Fenster, Türen, Löcher, Tunnel setzen Grenzen und öffnen Passagen. Die meist dunkle Rahmung fasst sie und betont den Übergang von einem Bereich zu einem anderen. Nicht alles ist zu sehen. Der Ausschnitt konzentriert den Blick. Unsere Neugier, unsere Schaulust wird geweckt, zu sehen, was verborgen bleibt.

Wenn man die Treppe nach oben gegangen war, zeigte sich ebenfalls ein solcher Übergangsort. Wer aufmerksam hinsah, konnte herausfinden, dass im zweiten Video genau der Gang zu sehen war, in den man sehen konnte. Die verkleinerte Wiederholung zeigte einfach, was es dort oben zu sehen gab – und doch schien es etwas Anderes, Geheimnisvolleres.

Paz richtet unsere Aufmerksamkeit auch dann auf den Raum zwischen Bild und Bildwiedergabe, wenn sie ihn nicht durch eine Schattenchoreographie bespielt. Die Bewegung der Schatten aber macht den sonst neutralen Raum als Handlungsraum erfahrbar. Durch die Akteure, die mit ihren Körpern die Bildprojektion unterbrechen, wird er zum Transformationsraum. Auf der Projektionsfläche erscheint diese Unterbrechung als mediale Schichtung.

Filmbild und Schattenspiel sind aufeinander bezogen. Weil sie aber zwei unterschiedlichen Repräsentationsebenen angehören, bleiben sie für den Betrachter zugleich getrennt. Die Differenz öffnet einen Raum, der auf den realen Raum zwischen Bild und Projektion verweist. Er kann für Reflexionen und Interventionen genutzt werden.

[1] Plinius Secundus d. Ä., „Die Tochter des Butades", in: *Naturkunde*, Bd. XXXV, hrsg. von Roderich König, Gerhard Winkler, Zürich 1997, S. 115.
[2] Alfréd Radok entwickelte das erste Programm als tschechischen Beitrag für die Weltausstellung 1958 in Brüssel.

Credits

01.
BLIND SPOTS
VIDEO, INSTALLATION — 2016

Concept, video, sound, and editing: Sharon Paz
Video performance: Matthias Alber, Elke Cybulski, Camilla Milena Fehér, Danielle Ana Füglistaller, Andreas A. Müller, Jürgen Salzmann, Karl-Heinz Stenz, Sabine Trötschel
Music: Tobias Vethake
Supported by: The National Lottery Council for the Arts, Israel
Exhibition: Raumlektüre, KulturRaum Zwingli-Kirche, Berlin, July 2016
Curator: Karin Scheel

02.
MARKS OF EXISTENCE
VIDEO, INSTALLATION — 2015

Concept, video, sound, and editing: Sharon Paz
In collaboration with: Jürgen Salzmann
Video performance: Matthias Alber, Elke Cybulski, Camilla Milena Fehér, Danielle Ana Füglistaller, Anne Sophie Malmberg, Andreas Albert Müller, Jürgen Salzmann, Karl-Heinz Stenz, Sabine Trötschel
Supported by: Goethe-Institut Israel, Mamuta Art and Media Center, Hansen House, Jerusalem Film Festival, Ostrovsky Foundation and Manofim Festival
Exhibition: Marks of Existence, Hansen House, Jerusalem, October 2015
Curator: Sala-Manca Group

03.
SINKING LAND
VIDEO, INSTALLATION — 2015

Concept, video, sound, and editing: Sharon Paz
In collaboration with: Jürgen Salzmann
Video performance: Matthias Alber, Elke Cybulski, Camilla Milena Fehér, Danielle Ana Füglistaller, Anne Sophie Malmberg, Andreas Albert Müller, Jürgen Salzmann, Karl-Heinz Stenz, Sabine Trötschel
Supported by: Goethe-Institut Israel, Mamuta Art and Media Center, Hansen House, Jerusalem Film Festival, Ostrovsky Foundation and Manofim Festival
Exhibition: Marks of Existence, Hansen House, Jerusalem, October 2015
Curator: Sala-Manca Group

04.
BEHIND THE WALL
VIDEO, PERFORMANCE — 2015

Concept, video, and editing: Sharon Paz
In collaboration with: Jürgen Salzmann and Theaterwerkstatt Hannover
Video performance: Matthias Alber, Elke Cybulski, Danielle Ana Füglistaller, Jürgen Salzmann, Sabine Trötschel
Live performance: Jürgen Salzmann, Benjamin Jagendorf
Music: Firas Roby, Sharon Paz
Supported by: Theaterwerkstatt Hannover, Goethe-Institut Israel, Mamuta Art and Media Center, Hansen House, Jerusalem Film Festival, Ostrovsky Foundation and Manofim Festival
Premiere: Unfortunately It Was Paradise oder liegenbleibende Wurstbrote, Theaterwerkstatt Hannover, January 2015

05.
WE FORGOT
VIDEO, PERFORMANCE — 2015

Concept, video, and editing: Sharon Paz
In collaboration with Cultura e.V.: Danielle Ana Füglistaller, Jürgen Salzmann, Karl-Heinz Stenz
Video performance: Danielle Ana Füglistaller, Jürgen Salzmann, Karl-Heinz Stenz
Live performance: Danielle Ana Füglistaller, Jürgen Salzmann, Karl-Heinz Stenz
Music: Tobias Vethake
Co-production: Forum Freies Theater (FFT) Düsseldorf and studiobühneköln
Supported by: Kulturamt der Landeshauptstadt Düsseldorf and Kulturamt der Stadt Köln
Premiere: We Forgot, FFT Düsseldorf, March 2015

06.
OPEN | CLOSE
VIDEO, INSTALLATION — 2014

Concept, video, sound, and editing: Sharon Paz
Video performance: Camilla Milena Fehér, Danielle Ana Füglistaller, Jürgen Salzmann, Karl-Heinz Stenz
Assistance: Karl-Heinz Stenz
Supported by: Stiftung Kulturwerk – VG Bild-Kunst, Bonn
Exhibition: Personal Territories, OKK/Raum29, Berlin, September 2014
Curators: Kerstin Karge and Sharon Paz

07.
PARALYZED MOVEMENT
VIDEO, INSTALLATION — 2014

Concept, video, and editing: Sharon Paz
Video performance: Camilla Milena Fehér, Danielle Ana Füglistaller, Jürgen Salzmann, Karl-Heinz Stenz
Music: Tobias Vethake
Assistance: Avi Revivo
Supported by: The Naggar School of Art, Musrara, Jerusalem
Exhibition: Analog – Epilog, Musrara Mix Festival 14, Jerusalem, May 2014
Curator: Sharon Horodi

08.
RESTRAINING MOTION 2014
VIDEO, INSTALLATION

Concept, video, and editing: Sharon Paz
Video performance: Camilla Milena Fehér,
Carolina Hellsgård, Amnon Liberman, Adi
Liraz, Dovrat Meron, Petra Spielhagen,
Karl-Heinz Stenz
Music: Tobias Vethake
Assistance: Karl-Heinz Stenz
Supported by: Stiftung Zurückgeben and
Verein zur Förderung von Kunst und Kultur
am Rosa-Luxemburg-Platz e.V., Berlin
Exhibition: *Restraining Motion*, Verein zur
Förderung von Kunst und Kultur am Rosa-
Luxemburg-Platz e.V., Berlin, January
2014
Curator: Susanne Prinz

09.
THE RIGHT TO LEAVE 2013
VIDEO

Concept, video, and editing: Sharon Paz
Video performance: Camilla Milena Fehér,
Jürgen Salzmann, Karl-Heinz Stenz
Music: Tobias Vethake
Supported by: Stiftung Zurückgeben and
Verein zur Förderung von Kunst und Kultur
am Rosa-Luxemburg-Platz e.V., Berlin
Exhibition: *Restraining Motion*, Verein zur
Förderung von Kunst und Kultur am Rosa-
Luxemburg-Platz e.V., Berlin, January
2014
Curator: Susanne Prinz

10.
SHADED WINDOWS 2012
VIDEO, PERFORMANCE

Concept, video, and editing: Sharon Paz
Video performance: Camilla Milena Fehér,
Jürgen Salzmann, Karl-Heinz Stenz
Live performance: Camilla Milena Fehér,
Jürgen Salzmann, Karl-Heinz Stenz
Music: Tobias Vethake
Supported by: Senatsverwaltung für
Kultur, Berlin
Exhibition: *Shaded Windows*, Pavillon am
Milchhof, Berlin, November 2012

11.
NO WALLS 2013
PUBLIC INSTALLATION

Concept: Sharon Paz
Supported by: nGbK, Berlin
Exhibition: *After Work, Art on the
Underground – Kunst im Untergrund*,
Bernauer Straße, U8
In cooperation with: nGbK, Berlin, June
2013
Curator: Uwe Jonas

12.
THE KING IS BLIND 2011
VIDEO, PERFORMANCE

Concept, video, and editing: Sharon Paz
In collaboration with: Danielle Ana
Füglistaller, Jürgen Salzmann, Karl-Heinz
Stenz, Ylva Jangsell
Video performance: Danielle Ana
Füglistaller, Gabriel Guler, Jürgen
Salzmann, Karl-Heinz Stenz, Benjamin
Jegendorf, Ylva Jangsell
Live performance: Danielle Ana
Füglistaller, Jürgen Salzmann, Karl-Heinz
Stenz, Ylva Jangsell
Music: Tobias Vethake
Supported by: Niedersächsisches
Ministerium für Wissenschaft und Kultur,
Stiftung Niedersachsen and Sparkasse
Hildesheim
Premiere: *Ansturm*, Hafen Hildesheim, May
2011

Special Thanks

Cultura e.V.: Karin Böttger, Danielle Ana
Füglistaller, Jürgen Salzmann, Karl-Heinz
Stenz / Dörte Ilsabé Dennemann / Juan
Pablo Diaz / DOCK 11: Wibke Janssen,
Kirsten Seeligmüller, Asier Solana, DOCK
11 Team / Eidotech Team / Camilla Milena
Fehér / Forum Freies Theater Düsseldorf:
Christoph Rech, Kathrin Tiedemann, FFT
Düsseldorf Team / Goethe-Institut Israel:
Dr. Wolf Iro, Goethe-Institut Team / Bikorey
Haitim / Hansen House Team / Pablo
Hermann / Stine Hollmann / Paula Hudson /
Uwe Jonas / Kerstin Karge / Amnon
Liberman / Kai Lorenz / Manofim: Rinat
Edelstein, Lee he Shulov / Medienwerkstatt
Berlin: Sandra Becker, Lioba von den
Driesch / Andreas Albert Müller / Musrara
Mix Festival: Sharon Horodi, Saron Paz,
Avi Sabag, Shlomit Yaacov, Musrara Mix
Festival Team / Pavillon am Milchhof:
Lindy Annis, Mariel Poppe, Pavillon am
Milchhof Team / Paz Family / Susanne
Prinz / Matthias Reichelt / REH Kunst:
Marie Arleth Skov / Sala-Manca Group:
Lea Mauas and Diego Rotman / Karin
Scheel / Miriam Sandra Schneider /
Petra Spielhagen / Efrat Stempler /
studiobühneköln: Dietmar Kobboldt,
studiobühneköln Team / Studio 44 Berlin /
THEATERDOCK Berlin / Theaterwerkstatt
Hannover: Matthias Alber, Elke Cybulski,
Sabine Trötschel / Ran Yaakoby / Judith
Weber

Biography

Born in Ramat-Gan, Israel
Lives and works in Berlin

EDUCATION

1997–2000 MFA Studio Program, Hunter College, New York
1994–1996 Independent Study Program, Beit Berl College
of Art, Kfar Saba, Israel
1990–1994 Bachelor of Science in Technical Education
(B.Sc.Te) and Teaching Diploma in Design,
Holon Institute of Technology, sponsored by
Tel Aviv University

PERFORMANCES

2015 *We Forgot*, DOCK11, Berlin
We Forgot, Forum Freies Theater (FFT) Düsseldorf
and studiobühneköln, Köln
2011 *The King is Blind*, 100 Grad Berlin 2011,
Sophiensäle and Loock Galerie, Berlin
The King is Blind, Hafen Hildesheim, collaboration
project with Cultura e.V., Hildesheim
2008 *Be-Longing*, Kulturwochen Nahost – radius of
art, KulturForum Kiel
2007 *Be-Longing*, Acco Festival of Alternative Theatre,
Acco, Israel and Nisoy Kelim, Tel Aviv
2005 *How Long*, DOCK11, Berlin

SOLO EXHIBITIONS

2017 *Homesick*, uqbar, Berlin
2015 *Marks of Existence*, Hansen House, Jerusalem
2014 *Restraining Motion*, Verein zur Förderung von
Kunst und Kultur am Rosa-Luxemburg-Platz e.V.,
Berlin
2013 *NO WALLS* – After Work, Art on the Underground
– Kunst im Untergrund, nGbK, Berlin
2012 *Shaded Windows*, Pavillon am Milchhof, Berlin
2009 *Is This a Good Day to Start a War*, arttransponder,
Berlin
2003 *Wandering Home*, Herzliya Museum of
Contemporary Art, Herzliya, Israel
2001 *And I Feel That I Just Got Home*, Peer Gallery,
Tel Aviv

GROUP EXHIBITIONS (SELECTED)

2017 *Constructing the Earthquake*, Galerie im
Körnerpark, Berlin
2016 *Raumlektüre*, KulturRaum Zwingli-Kirche, Berlin
Heimat – Identifikation im Wandel, Künstlerverein
Walkmühle, Wiesbaden
Auki/Open/Öppen, Video Art Festival Turku –
VAFT, Turku, Finland
2015 *My Horizontal Is Your Vertical*, Scotty Enterprises,
Berlin
RoundAbout, ID Festival Berlin, Radialsystem V,
Berlin
2014 *Personal Territories*, OKK/Raum29, Berlin
Analog – Epilog, Musrara Mix Festival 14,
Jerusalem in dialogue, City Gallery des
Kunstverein Wolfsburg
Doh Mix Meh Up, Oxford Diasporas Programme,
Old Fire Station, Oxford, UK
2013 *Panorama*, Weserburg Museum für moderne
Kunst, Bremen
2011 *Fast and Furious*, Goldrausch 2011, Halle am
Wasser, Berlin
2010 *Video Zone*, 5th International Video Art Biennial,
Tel Aviv
2009 *Thy Brothers' Keeper*, Kulturverein Zehntscheuer
e.V., Rottenburg
2008 *The Mirror Stage*, Independent Museum of
Contemporary Art – IMCA, Limassol, Cyprus
2007 *Engagement*, Israel-Museum, Jerusalem
2006 *Disruptions*, Detach Tikva Museum of Art, Petach
Tikva, Israel
Legal Aliens, Smack Mellon, New York
Restless: Photography and New Media, The
Museum of Contemporary Art Shanghai
Art of Living, The Contemporary Jewish Museum,
San Francisco
2004 *From Inside and Outside*, ZKMax, München
*New Exposures: Recent Acquisitions in
Photography*, Israel-Museum, Jerusalem
INNENraeumeAUSSENstaedte, ZKM Medialounge,
Karlsruhe
2002 *Blinder*Codes #1992–2002*, Staatliche Akademie

der Bildenden Künste, Karlsruhe
New Views, Open Studios Exhibition, DUMBO, New York
AIM 22, The Bronx Museum of the Arts, New York
Brooklyn à Paris, Espace Huit Novembre Centre d'Art, Paris
Dangerous Beauty, JCC Manhattan, New York
ArtAttack Project, Gwangju Biennale, Gwangju, South Korea

2001   *Vacancy*, Star 67, New York
2000   *Rocking House*, MFA Thesis Show, Hunter College, New York

VIDEO FESTIVALS AND SCREENINGS (SELECTED)

2016   *Hivhov*, Video Art Festival, Jerusalem
       Divisions, Skowhegan Alumni Video Screening, New York
2015   *Homemade 4*, Vernon Gallery, Prague
2014   *The Israeli Video Art Awards*, Jerusalem International Film Festival, Jerusalem
2012   *Tape Modern No. 25*, Tape Modern, Berlin
2011   *Homemade 4*, Loop Festival, Barcelona
       This is a Good Day to Start a War, transmediale – Festival for Art and Digital Culture, Berlin
2008   *About the City*, Galapagos Art Space, DUMBO Festival, New York
2006   *Cut and Paste – New Identities*, New Territories, Makor, New York
2004   *Homemade 2*, The Center for Contemporary Art – Ujazdowski Castle, Warsaw
2003   The 1st Transmanchurian Video Festival, Beijing
2002   *MOOV*, White Box, New York
       The Dialog, Thomas Erben Gallery, New York
       Contaminados, Museum of Contemporary Art and Design, San José, Costa Rica
       My Double and Its Double, Images Festival, Toronto
2001   *Video Marathon*, Art in General, New York
       D.U.M.B.O. Short Film and Video Festival, New York
       Media Forum, XXIII. Moscow International Film Festival, Moscow

AWARDS AND FELLOWSHIPS

2016   *New Media and Installation Project Fund*, Israel National Lottery Council for the Arts
2015   *Künstlerinnenprogramm*, Senatsverwaltung für Kultur, Berlin
       Project Grand, Goethe-Institut, Israel
2014   *The Israeli Video Art and Experimental Cinema Award*, Jerusalem International Film Festival

2013   *HIAP Residency*, Helsinki, Finland
2012   *Projektstipendium*, Senatsverwaltung für Kultur, Berlin
2010   *Goldrausch Künstlerinnenprojekt*, Berlin
2009   *Israel National Lottery Council for the Arts arttransponder Project Grand*, Berlin
2008   *The Israeli Fund for Video Art and Experimental Cinema*
2007   *The Rabinovitch Foundation for the Arts*, Israel
       Israel National Lottery Council for the Arts
2005   *Residency Programme*, Irish Museum of Modern Art, Ireland
2004   *Hauptstadtkulturfonds*, Berlin
2002   *New Views – DUMBO Residency*, The Lower Manhattan Cultural Council, New York
2002   *Artist in the Marketplace Program*, The Bronx Museum of the Arts, New York
2001   *Skowhegan School of Painting and Sculpture Fellowship*, New York
       50 Best, CTRL[SPACE], \\international\media\ art award 2001, ZKM, Karlsruhe

COLLECTIONS

Neuer Berliner Kunstverein, Video-Forum, Berlin
Israel-Museum, Jerusalem
The Brandes Family Art Collection, Tel Aviv
Guy and Marion Naggar, London

PUBLICATIONS (SELECTED)

2016   *Heimat – Identifikation im Wandel*, Künstlerverein Walkmühle, Wiesbaden
2014   *Personal Territories*, OKK/Raum29, Berlin
2013   *NO WALLS – After Work*, Art on the Underground – Kunst im Untergrund, nGbK, Berlin
2011   *The King is Blind*, Goldrausch Künstlerinnenprojekt, Berlin
2009   *Is This a Good Day to Start a War*, arttransponder, Berlin
2007   *Be-Longing*, Goethe-Institut, Tel Aviv
2006   *Disruptions: Life in a Threatened Space*, Petach Tikva Museum of Art, Petach Tikva, Israel
       Thy Brothers' Keeper, Flint Institute of Arts, Flint, USA
2005   *How Long*, Hauptstadtkulturfonds, Berlin
2002   *AIM 22*, The Bronx Museum of the Arts, New York
       Video Artist, Dangerous Beauty, JCC Manhattan, New York
2001   *50 Best*, CTRL[SPACE], \\international\media\ art award 2001, ZKM, Karlsruhe

Conception
Sharon Paz

Text
Ines Lindner

Introduction/Synopses
Angelika Richter

Translation
(German – English)
Brian Currid

German copy editing
Christine Woditschka

English copy editing
Jane Michael

Graphic Design
DAS MOMENT, Berlin

Printing
Druckerei Conrad, Berlin

Edition
500 copies

Photo credits
Klaus Fleige (p. 118)
Andreas Hartmann (p. 119)
Snir Katzir (pp. 37, 38, 39)
Adi Liraz (pp. 80, 99)
Ludger Paffrath (pp. 78, 81, 82, 83, 91)
Sharon Paz (pp. 12–36, 42–77)
Petra Spielhagen (pp. 98, 100, 102, 110, 111)

Published by
✳ argobooks, Berlin
Choriner Straße 57
10435 Berlin
Germany
Ph. +49 (0)30 41 72 56 31
www.argobooks.de

ISBN 978-3-942700-82-5

Printed in Germany

The catalog was supported by
Senatsverwaltung für Kultur, Berlin
Israel National Lottery Council for the Arts